RACING HEARTS

Our eyes locked, and without a word I kicked my feet out of the stirrups and slid to the ground. I wanted to keep looking into his eyes, but my legs were turning to jelly under me, and I suddenly felt shy. So I busied myself unbuckling the girth of the saddle.

All of a sudden I felt Paul's hands on my neck and shoulders, massaging my aching muscles as though he knew exactly where they hurt. I was too thrilled to speak. His hands felt so warm and gentle. Everything else was blurry around me. All I could focus on was the touch of his hands. His fingertips moved lightly up my neck to my scalp, and I tilted my head forward. I couldn't believe anything could feel so good.

"Barrie?" Paul's voice was husky behind me, and I slowly turned around. I was sure he was going to kiss me, and I knew it was going to be wonderful. I raised my head and gazed deep into those gorgeous brown eyes. . . .

Bantam Sweet Dreams Romances
Ask your bookseller for the books you have missed

#1   P.S. I LOVE YOU
#169 GOLDEN GIRL
#170 ROCK 'N' ROLL
      SWEETHEART
#171 ACTING ON IMPULSE
#172 SUN KISSED
#173 MUSIC FROM THE
      HEART

#174 LOVE ON STRIKE
#175 PUPPY LOVE
#176 WRONG-WAY
      ROMANCE
#177 THE TRUTH ABOUT
      LOVE
#178 PROJECT BOYFRIEND
#179 RACING HEARTS

Sweet Dreams

RACING HEARTS
SUSAN SLOATE

BANTAM BOOKS
NEW YORK · TORONTO · LONDON · SYDNEY · AUCKLAND

RL 6, age 11 and up

RACING HEARTS
A Bantam Book / May 1991

*Bantam Books are published by Bantam Books, a division
of Bantam Doubleday Dell Publishing Group, Inc. Its trademark, consisting of the words "Bantam Books" and the
portrayal of a rooster, is Registered in U.S. Patent and
Trademark Office and in other countries. Marca Regis-
trada. Bantam Books, 666 Fifth Avenue, New York, New
York 10103.*

PRINTED IN THE UNITED STATES OF AMERICA

OPM   0 9 8 7 6 5 4 3 2 1

*To the World Jockey Association
Racing School, with love and thanks*

Chapter One

"They're to die for! Oh, Barrie, they're *gorgeous,*" my best friend Julie Fredericks exclaimed, nudging me as we stared at the shoes displayed in the window of our favorite boutique. The whole display was amazing, but Julie and I were both staring at one pair of shoes in particular.

That's how it is with Julie and me. One of the reasons we're best friends is because we like the same clothes and jewelry and sometimes even the same boys. (Luckily, we've never fought over the same guy.) It's nice to know that when I think something is cute, Julie does, too.

Of course, we have our differences. For example, I just had to try on those beautiful silver-strapped dancing shoes. Julie thought they were incredible, too, but it would never have occurred to her to actually buy them. She didn't really need them. Julie would

1

think of them as just a fabulous luxury for somebody else.

In a few minutes one of the salesgirls brought over a pair of the sandals in my size, and I put them on. I twirled in front of the mirror, admiring the way the shoes made me seem taller and more exotic. The lights around the full-length mirror brought out the chestnut highlights in my hair, which is long, brown, and curly, and picked up the sparkle in my green eyes.

"You're not really going to buy them, are you?" Julie said as I checked out the box for the price tag.

"And what's wrong," I retorted, "with buying an item that . . . " My voice trailed off. I'd just caught a glimpse of the price. *That* was what was wrong! At that price the shoes would soak up most of the money I'd saved over the last six months.

Oh, but I had to have them! I could already picture myself at The Club, our town's hottest dance spot, with dozens of tall, dark, and handsome boys all fighting to dance with me. It was a great fantasy. I have to admit that my fantasies usually get the better of my sensible side. Face it—my sensible side just doesn't fight back very hard.

Julie's, on the other hand, is fully developed. "Barrie Sampson, are you crazy? All that money for one pair of shoes? Your parents will think you've flipped out completely!"

2

I was admiring the way the buckles on my toes caught the light. "Come on, Julie, loosen up. Don't you realize these shoes are part of the strategy?"

"What strategy?"

"*My* strategy. The strategy that'll help me find *him*."

"Him who?"

Sometimes Julie is so dense, I can't believe it. *"Him,"* I repeated. "That big, gorgeous hunk who's been waiting for me to come into his life. When he sees me in these shoes, Julie, it's Cinderella time!"

"Better check the shoes again," Julie said dryly. "They don't look like glass to me."

I carefully took off the shoes and set them back in their tissue-paper nest. "Listen, Julie, I can feel it in my bones. This is the summer that it happens. Maybe at The Club or on the beach or wherever, but he'll take one look at me, and that will be it. By Labor Day we'll be head over heels in love."

Julie glanced doubtfully at the shoe box as I gave it to the salesgirl and dug into my purse. "All because of a pair of shoes?"

"They're not just shoes. They're glamorous and sophisticated, and they'll make me that way." I handed the salesgirl all the bills in my wallet. "And they're worth every dime. I'll be wearing them all summer long."

That's what I thought, anyway. But at dinner that night, I found out I was wrong.

Normally my parents are the best in the world. They've always trusted me and been nice to my friends and given permission when I wanted to do something special, like the summer I spent two weeks camping with my friends when I was twelve. When it's really important, I can always count on them to see my side of things.

So it was a shock when I showed off my new shoes and neither of them said anything. "Don't you like them?" I asked.

"Barrie . . ." My dad cleared his throat. "We—uh—we've been talking about this summer. And we just don't think it's a terrific idea for you to stay here in town."

"What? Where else should I be?" For one wild moment I thought they might be considering sending me on some glamorous cruise, or maybe even on a trip to Europe.

No such luck. "Your aunt Christy called a few days ago," Mom explained. "She and Harv would love to have you spend the summer on their farm."

"Their *farm?*" I couldn't believe it. Although Christy and Harv lived only eighty miles away from us, their rural lifestyle made them seem as if they lived on another planet. "You've got to be kidding."

"You've always been crazy about your aunt and uncle," Dad pointed out.

"Well, sure. They're the greatest. But they work like slaves all day long." I was starting to feel very alarmed. "I'll never get to wear my new shoes anywhere, and what kind of guys could I meet out there? If I go to Connecticut, my whole summer's ruined!"

I saw my parents look at each other, which was a bad sign. That usually meant they'd been talking about me. Whatever was coming was probably unpleasant, and I wasn't looking forward to hearing it.

What it came down to was my report card, which had arrived in the mail just before I got home from the mall. I usually get pretty good grades, but my teachers are always telling me and my parents that I'd do a lot better if I just applied myself a little more. To be honest, I'd rather apply myself to having fun. Slaving away at trig problems and history papers definitely isn't my idea of a good time. So I always got my work done, but I did it fast, so I could hang out with Julie and my other friends as soon as possible.

Dad was looking down at the report card in his hand. He usually stood up for me when I wanted to do something Mom thought was outrageous. We've always been pretty close. But now he looked as stern as Mom did.

I peeked over his shoulder. I'd gotten C's in both trig and history, and I knew that with a little more work, I could have gotten B's. "Sorry, guys," I mumbled. "I guess I could've done better."

Mom nodded. "That's why we want you to

spend some time at the farm. Christy's a lot of fun, but she's also disciplined and organized. You'll learn a lot from her about being responsible."

I couldn't believe this was happening. It was like something out of one of those old *Twilight Zone* episodes on late-night TV. My glamorous, hunk-filled summer was turning into a rural, boyless nightmare. I couldn't even stand to think about it!

I spent the next two weeks trying to change my parents' minds. I offered to get a summer job in town or give up my five-day-a-week stint at the beach or even limit my time at The Club. It didn't work. They'd decided that I had to stop partying and get serious. My arguments didn't stand a chance. My sixteenth summer, which I'd looked forward to for months, was going to be a total washout.

Two days after school ended, Julie and I waited together for the train that would take me away from civilization. Julie had driven me to the station because Mom and Dad were both at work.

"It can't be all that bad," Julie said consolingly as the train pulled up to the platform. "You're always telling me how much fun Christy is and how much you like visiting her and Harv."

I eyed the train gloomily. "They're terrific.

But what about that big, gorgeous hunk I was looking for?"

"Maybe he'll show up in Connecticut," Julie said hopefully.

"Where? Under a haystack? That's the only place I'd ever see him." I tried to smile, but it was tough. When the train whistle sounded, I knew I couldn't stall any longer. "Oh, well. There goes my summer," I sighed. I hugged Julie good-bye and boarded the train. As I sat down, I thought about my brand-new silver-strapped dancing shoes. At the last minute I'd stuffed them into my suitcase. You never knew. A hunk might be hiding just about anyplace, even under a haystack.

Christy was standing on the railroad platform as my train pulled in. She was wearing faded jeans and a pale pink polo shirt that showed off her golden tan. A pair of oversized sunglasses were pushed up on top of her long brown hair. I couldn't help grinning at the sight of her. She looked great. If it weren't for her wedding ring and the air of command that I'd always liked, Christy might have been mistaken for one of the gang at school. She was my dad's younger sister, but she was too young and fun for me ever to call her Aunt. I just thought of her as Christy, one of my very best friends.

"Hey, Barrie! You look like you've already

started working on your tan." Christy gave me a big hug as I stepped onto the platform.

I laughed. "And I can tell I'll be working on a lot more than that this summer!"

We chattered all the way home in her Jeep. When I filled her in on my less-than-perfect report card, Christy shrugged. "Hey, it happens. I know you weren't goofing off."

"But I was," I admitted sadly. "And this"— I waved at the farm coming into view—"is how I'm paying for it."

As soon as the words were out, I realized how awful they sounded. I tried to apologize, but Christy waved it off. "Don't worry about it. I know what you meant. And hey, we have a lot of different chores around here. You can pick what you want to do." She smiled slyly. "You might even help me with the horses, if you want."

Christy knew very well that I loved horses and loved to ride. If I had to be stuck doing farm work, I'd rather it was farm work that involved horses. Suddenly things looked a little brighter.

It was still dark the next morning when I heard voices and a rap on the door of my bedroom. "Rise and shine, honey!" Harv called.

Rise and shine? It was barely dawn! I pulled the blanket over my head and tried to settle back to sleep. *It's a nightmare*, I told myself. *A mistake. Go back to sleep.*

"Let's go, Barrie." This time it was Christy—and she was in my room, shaking my shoulder so I couldn't possibly ignore her. "Let's exercise those horses."

"Glug," I mumbled.

"Does that mean yes?"

I don't know how I did it, but fifteen minutes later I was outside, breathing in the crisp morning air. Christy introduced me to her two horses, a beautiful bay mare named Plum Rose and a sleek gray horse, Harvey's Girl. We fed and groomed the horses while Harv took care of the other early-morning chores.

"You two can exercise them at the Rolling Meadows racetrack down the road," Harv told me as I finished brushing down the horses. "And when you and Christy get back, we'll have a big breakfast together."

"Take Plum Rose," Christy suggested. "She's pretty gentle, and I think you'll do fine with her."

I'd forgotten how much I missed riding. There was a stable near my home, but I hadn't been there in a while. When I swung myself from the mounting block into the saddle, I suddenly felt completely content. Next to kissing the boy of my dreams, a good gallop on a fast horse has always been my idea of heaven. Even if it's not very glamorous, it sure is fun.

A few minutes later we were on our way.

Christy, riding beside me on Harvey's Girl, directed me to turn into a wide driveway. The sign in front read Rolling Meadows Jockey School, and a bridle path led directly to the track.

"Wow, this is great!" I stared at the large, well-kept oval, fenced in with neat white rails. It all looked so professional. "You ride here every day?"

"Every day." Christy smiled. "We're friendly with the guy who runs this place. And if you like, you and I can ride here all summer long. Tough chore, huh?"

I was too happy to answer. If riding and caring for beautiful horses every day was my parents' idea of taking responsibility, it was okay with me! Even if no gorgeous hunk figured in the picture, it was still pretty wonderful.

"We canter them around the track a couple of times," Christy told me as we walked the horses out on the track.

"Okay," I agreed. "Let's go." I started Plum Rose down the path.

"Hold it, Barrie. I want to adjust this stirrup leather," Christy said.

"It's okay," I called back reassuringly from the track. I was anxious to start off on my own. "I'll take Plum Rose around once myself."

"You shouldn't be riding alone," Christy insisted.

"I'm not alone," I laughed. "You're right here. What could possibly happen?"

I didn't hear any answer from Christy, so I signaled Plum Rose to trot. Then, when she was trotting nicely, I applied my whole leg to her side. In a moment she broke stride gently and rocked into a soft canter.

Everything felt just fine. The air was summery soft, and the sun was just peeking over the mountains. I took a deep breath, feeling Plum Rose moving nicely under me. Coming to Connecticut wasn't the worst thing in the world after all.

Then it happened. I heard a thunder of hooves behind me, and a streak of white flashed by on my right. It was another horse and rider, and Plum Rose whinnied in protest. In a moment her canter turned into a headlong gallop, her speed increasing with every stride.

I tried to slow her down, but it was hopeless. Plum Rose had the bit in her teeth, and she bolted right down the track as I held onto the saddle in a panic. I knew I should talk to the horse and calm her to a walk, but I couldn't manage to say a word. I was terrified. If I fell off at that speed, who knew what might happen?

"Whoa, girl. Easy." I heard a male voice beside me over the pounding hoofbeats of his horse and mine, but I was so busy just hanging on, I didn't dare turn my head. Plum

Rose was still galloping madly, and I was concentrating all my attention on staying in the saddle.

"Slow down, girl. Slow . . . slow . . ." The voice stayed steady and calm, soothing the mare, while a strong hand reached out to take hold of my reins.

To my relief Plum Rose actually began to listen to the calm voice. Her speed slackened bit by bit, and in a few moments she slowed down to a walk.

"Thatta girl." The voice was approving now. "I knew you could do it. No need to be scared. Everything's fine." The hand reached out again, this time to pat the horse's neck.

I was shaking all over. I'd never been so scared in my life. Slowly, still afraid to turn my head, I pulled on the reins and whispered, "Whoa, girl." Plum Rose stopped instantly, right in the middle of the track. Finally I could risk a look at the person behind the soothing voice.

When I saw him, I nearly gasped. Talk about daydreams coming true! I was staring at the best-looking guy I'd seen in ages. He was even sitting on a white horse! The guy smiled at me, and my heart, which had begun to slow down to normal, started racing again. He had a wonderful, warm smile and equally wonderful, warm, deep brown eyes that crinkled at the corners. He looked as if he were enjoying himself. "Scared?" he asked.

"To death," I admitted, trying hard not to stare—or faint. What a hunk. "I thought Plum Rose was supposed to be gentle."

"Barrie, are you all right?" Christy cantered up behind us on Harvey's Girl, her face anxious and strained. I'd never seen her so upset.

"She's fine," my rescuer assured her before she could speak. He turned to me. "Anything hurt?"

"I—I don't think so." What was the matter with me? Why couldn't I think of anything brilliant to say?

He grinned again. "You look like you're okay. At least, you look pretty good to me." He touched his riding helmet in salute. "So long," he said as his horse trotted off.

"Hey, thanks!" I called after him. It was all I could think of to say. What I really wanted to do was ask him about his entire life history, including his most recent romantic encounters. But I figured I wouldn't be able to get all that into one sentence, and anyway, he didn't even look back. I must have made some great impression.

"Barrie, are you *sure* you're all right?" Christy asked again, riding up beside me.

I stared after my mysterious knight on horseback. "Do you know him?"

Christy grinned, her face the picture of relief. "I guess you must be okay if you're asking questions like that. That's Paul Kaufman. I've met him here a few times. He works at Rolling Meadows as a stable assistant, I think. He's about seventeen, and he seems to be a great guy. *Now* do you feel all right?"

I strained for a last glimpse of Paul's broad, sturdy shoulders and straight back. Then I turned to Christy with my biggest, most radiant smile. "I feel just fine!"

Chapter Two

"But, Dad, this takes a lot of responsibility!" I protested over the phone two nights later. "Isn't that what you and Mom wanted?"

I could hear Christy giggling behind me as she cleared the dinner table. Harv was trying to muffle his chuckles behind the newspaper. I turned and glared at both of them.

"Honest, Dad, I've thought about this a lot," I insisted. I had, too. I'd spent a lot of sleepless hours remembering the boy with the gorgeous dark eyes and warm smile. I'd also read through the entire brochure from Rolling Meadows Jockey School about a dozen times. It was true I'd been looking for Paul Kaufman's picture while I read it, but what I read sounded just great.

The brochure said that the students trained in small groups to become jockeys or exercise riders. The training included instruction in stable procedure, basic anatomy and medical care of horses, the proper use of jockey equipment like riding whips, hats, and boots, and of course, riding racehorses.

I loved the idea of it right away. I could learn how to be an exercise rider, a rider who rode horses at the track in the early mornings to keep the horses in condition. When I got back home, I could get a job as an exercise rider and work before school at Marlborough Racetrack, which was near my home. It would be a perfect way to earn extra money, stay in shape, and be around horses at the same time. Best of all, if I attended Rolling Meadows as a student, I'd see Paul Kaufman every single day. Of course, I didn't mention that part of the plan to my parents.

Dad and I talked for a long time. I had to promise him I'd be very careful when riding and follow all the stable instructions to the letter. I didn't tell him about my near disaster on Plum Rose the other day. I figured that Plum Rose was one of Christy's horses, not one that belonged to Rolling Meadows, so she didn't really count.

Dad asked to speak to Christy, who got her giggles under control before she came to the phone. After they talked for an even longer time, I spoke to Dad again. He agreed to pay my tuition at Rolling Meadows for the summer on the condition that I continue to stay with Christy and Harv instead of moving to the school dorm. I agreed immediately. I was so thrilled, I'd have agreed to anything as long as it meant I could get to know Paul!

Christy was still smiling when I finally hung up the phone. "Did you tell your dad you'd be going to school in the morning and going after a great-looking guy in the afternoon?" she teased.

"I won't be going after anybody," I defended myself. "But if the guy you're talking about just happens to find me attractive, that certainly wouldn't be my fault."

"Oh, no," Christy said solemnly, "it wouldn't. You'd only be up at four in the morning getting your makeup right."

I laughed at the time, but it was no joke a few days later, when my alarm clock woke me at five for my first morning's work at Rolling Meadows. That was *early*. For a minute I was really tempted to just turn over and go back to sleep. Then I remembered Paul Kaufman's brown eyes, and I dragged myself out of bed.

It was still dark when I got to the stables. I saw some of the other students standing around yawning, but there was no sign of Paul. As I stood there uncertainly, not knowing where to go or what to do, a pretty blond girl saw me and came over with a friendly smile.

"You're the new student, aren't you? Hi, I'm Marla Foster. Welcome to the ranks of the slaves."

"I'm Barrie Sampson," I said, feeling a little

awkward. Marla looked to be about my age, and she was very pretty. "Is that what it's really like?" I asked.

"What it's really like is army boot camp—with horses." Marla laughed.

"Ain't it the truth," said a guy who joined us. He grinned. "You'll have fun, though. We all do, every day." Marla introduced him as Greg. Then the other four students walked over. Counting Marla, Greg, and me, there were five girls and two boys altogether. Bobby was about seventeen, with sharp features and a sharper attitude. Tessa, fifteen, was obviously still fighting off the last traces of baby fat. Jo and Wendy were around my age. They were very friendly and funny. I noticed that everyone, guys and girls, was either my height or shorter.

All of them started shooting questions at me at once. How much riding experience did I have? Where was I from? Did I want to be a jockey or an exercise rider?

I was so busy answering them that I hardly noticed the boy who came out of the shed behind the stables. Then I turned to look at him. It was Paul Kaufman, and he was even more gorgeous than I'd remembered.

"Feed, everybody!" he called. "There are a lot of hungry horses waiting." The students went off in a rush, talking and laughing together. But I didn't know what I was supposed to do, so I just stood there. Besides, just *looking* at Paul floored me. He was wearing a soft gray sweatshirt over faded jeans and dusty black boots, and he looked terrific. But something seemed wrong. I realized that he looked a lot shorter than I'd remembered. The only time I'd ever seen him before, he was in the saddle, so I hadn't thought about his height. Face to face, though, he was no taller than I was—which is five feet six inches.

Paul saw me staring at him, and he gave me another of those amazing smiles. "Well, hi. So you're the new girl."

"That's me," I said, trying to sound light-hearted. *Brilliant comeback,* I thought. *Can't you do better than that?* Hastily I added, "My name's Barrie Sampson."

"Paul Kaufman," he answered. "Nice to have you here."

His smile was so warm that for just a second it sounded as if he meant those words in more than just a friendly kind of way. Could he have been thinking about me as much as I'd been thinking about him?

Then I remembered that I was here to work and to learn. "Uh—what am I supposed to do?" I asked. "Nobody's told me."

"Dutch—he runs the school—asked me to show you the ropes and kind of help you out," Paul explained. "So I'll work with you for today, all right?"

All right? My heart was singing as I thought, *Anything's all right if you're involved in it.*

I have no problem at all with that arrangement!

Three hours later I straightened up and wiped the sweat off my forehead. "You're doing fine," Paul said encouragingly. "Try it again."

I took a quick look down at myself and almost wilted with embarrassment. The brand-new regulation black boots I'd had to buy to wear at Rolling Meadows were already dusty. My shirt was streaked with grime. I could feel strands of my hair pulling out of the ponytail I'd fixed so carefully early that morning. I was afraid to even think of what my face looked like. *Some glamour girl,* I thought. *It's a miracle Paul hasn't died laughing at the sight of you!*

But when I glanced at him, he was looking at the horse stall I was mucking out with the long steel-tipped rake he'd used earlier to demonstrate the procedure. Now he watched as I scooped up a small load of hay, straw, and horse droppings. I tossed the load against the wall of the stall the way he had shown me, and the horse droppings fell to the bottom. Then I scooped them up and tossed them into a wheelbarrow.

"That's it," he said approvingly as I scooped and tossed, making a neat square near the door of the stall. "Now in the middle—" He showed me how to remove the soiled straw from the middle.

Ugh! When I'd read the brochure, I hadn't seen any mention of cleaning out horse stalls. In fact, when I thought about the other chores Paul had shown me how to do, I began to realize that none of them was mentioned in the brochure. As I tried to follow his directions, I began to wonder about my commitment. Horse racing as a profession suddenly looked a lot less glamorous than the brochure had described it.

"That's fine," Paul told me a while later, as I dumped a wheelbarrow's worth of fresh shavings on the neat square of clean straw in the stall. "You're picking it up like a pro."

Marla was passing by with her own overflowing wheelbarrow. "You won't believe it, Barrie, but that's a terrific compliment, coming from Paul."

"Really?" I looked hopefully at Paul. Was cleaning out a filthy stall the way to his heart?

Paul grinned at Marla. "She's doing great," he told her. "If we ever do a video on How to Muck out a Stall, Barrie ought to star in it."

"Now that's something to look forward to!" I laughed. Now that the stall was finished, I felt like resting for a moment. "How about taking a break?" I asked hopefully.

Paul glanced at his watch. "Sorry," he said cheerfully, "not for another hour or so. But don't worry. You won't get bored. There's plenty more to do."

He wasn't kidding, either. Rolling Meadows operated on a tight schedule, and everybody had to pitch in for the work to get done on time. Once the horses were fed in the morning, students were responsible for grooming and tacking them, that is, brushing them down, inspecting and wrapping their legs, and putting on their saddles and bridles. Then the advanced students rode the horses on the track, while the others, including me, mucked out stalls and helped unsaddle the horses when they returned from their workouts.

When the horses were finished being exercised, we tied them securely to the wash racks, washed and dried them, gave them water to drink, and wrapped their legs with bandages soaked in cold water to protect their delicate muscles. There was a funny-looking treelike contraption called a hot-walker that moved around in a circle, forcing the horses tied to it to keep walking. That kept their legs from stiffening up after their workout. When they came off the hot-walker, the horses were given hay to nibble on and then were led back to their stalls.

Meanwhile the students gathered all the cloths and leg wraps used in the morning, laundered each piece by hand, then hung them on a line behind the stable. We also had to clean and inspect all the tack every day. We checked the metal bits to be sure they were sturdy and looked over the girths and leather reins for any tears or fraying that might have developed. If anything was damaged, we told Paul about it, and he immediately repaired it. If tack broke while a horse was on the track, it could mean serious injury to both horse or rider.

By eleven o'clock I was so exhausted that I felt I had to either sit down or pass out. Paul had gone off to check on the medication for one of the horses, and everyone else was checking tack or hanging up laundry. I figured that everything was being taken care of, so I sat down on one of the benches near the wash rack.

"Hey, girl, up and at 'em!" barked a voice behind me. "Is that any way for a jockey to behave?"

I almost jumped out of my skin and angrily looked up for the source of the voice. Was I ever going to give that guy a piece of my mind!

The man regarding me was tall and slim, probably in his mid-forties, and had the kind of grin that could turn steely very quickly. He was wearing a pair of the oldest jeans I'd ever seen and a faded flannel shirt. As I just sat there, glaring at him, he ambled over. "You the new girl? I'm Dutch Callahan. This is my place."

"Well, I'm Barrie Sampson, and—" I began, intending to go a lot further. But Dutch stopped me with a wave of his hand.

"Honey, on my place you play by my rules. Now let's see you stand up. Thatta girl. Nobody sits down around the stable when there's work to be done. It's not professional."

"I'm not professional," I protested. "I'm just a student."

Dutch held up his hand again. "At Rolling Meadows we're all professionals. While you're here, you're gonna act like the most professional jockey in the business." He looked at his watch. " 'Course, this is your first day. And you haven't had your break yet. So you just run on up to the house and relax. You get a half hour off. Then get back here and boogie!"

A half hour? After working for five and a half hours, I got only a half hour off? I began to reconsider the jokes about slave labor that I'd heard all morning. Those guys weren't kidding!

There was a large wooden building behind the stables that served as a dormitory for the girls, and I headed toward it, hoping to stretch out for a while. My boots felt tight, and I could feel my toes cramping in the hot leather. I would have given anything to lie down for a few minutes.

Wendy and Jo were sipping sodas on the

shady back porch when I got there. In my rush to keep up with Paul, I'd hardly had a chance to talk to them at all. Now I felt awkward again as I walked up the steps to the porch.

It surprised me when both of them gave me friendly smiles and offered me a soda. "That'd be great," I said with feeling. "I can't believe how thirsty I got out there."

"It's like that every day," Jo said, handing me a cold can from an ice chest behind her. "The rule around here is, whenever you *do* get a break, *always* eat, *always* drink, and *always* go to the bathroom."

We all laughed, but I was still smarting over Dutch's remarks. Act professional? This was my summer vacation we were talking about! But before I could ask Jo and Wendy if Dutch was always like that, Wendy was asking me how the morning had gone. "Having fun?"

"Oh, sure," I told her wryly as I sank down on the porch steps. "It's been just swell."

Both of them obviously missed the sarcasm. "Good," Jo said enthusiastically. "Paul's such a good instructor. He makes things really easy, doesn't he?"

My ears perked up at the mention of his name. Of course, I wasn't about to tell someone I didn't know very well that my mind had been on Paul for days. Still, I wanted to know what the other girls thought of him. I tried to be subtle about it. "Has Paul been here a long time?" I asked casually.

Jo popped open a second soda can for herself. "About a year, part-time. He just graduated from high school, so now he's working full-time. And he rides better than anybody here. He'll probably make a super jockey."

"I know he will." Wendy tossed her empty can in the trash. She leaned toward me, bright blue eyes sparkling. "Have you taken a good look at him?"

Are you kidding? I thought. *I've done nothing but look at him whenever I had the chance!* But naturally I kept quiet.

Wendy went on, "I mean, he's built exactly right for a jockey—small and compact. And he's got a great temperament, too. He's real even-tempered. And man, can he concentrate!"

"He was very nice to me this morning," I said, hoping to get some more information. "Is he nice to everybody?"

"Oh, yeah," Wendy assured me. I hoped the expression on my face didn't give me away. I was hoping that Paul's friendliness meant he thought I was something . . . well, at least a little special.

I would have prodded them for more information but Jo looked behind me and chirped, "Hey, Paul, we were just talking about you!"

I could feel my face reddening, and I kept my back turned. The last thing I needed on my first day was for Paul to know how attractive I thought he was.

I heard him come up behind me, and the girls chatted easily with him as I tried to think of something to say. It was funny. I'd never had any trouble talking to a guy before, but somehow Paul made me feel completely tongue-tied. So I didn't say anything.

"Break's over, ladies," Paul told Wendy and Jo. "Get back out there and get your horses ready. You're riding next." He nudged me with his boot. "And *you're* coming along to watch. Up and at 'em!"

I turned my head to glare at him, but Paul's smile was irresistible. I couldn't help smiling back. As Wendy and Jo clumped down the steps, Paul reached out his hand to pull me to my feet. "Come on, rookie," he said with a grin. "Back to the grind."

For just a moment his warm hand held mine, and suddenly I didn't feel tired at all. In fact, I could have started the whole backbreaking day all over again. Could I possibly have fallen in love?

Chapter Three

"**H**ey, that hurts!" I groaned as Christy pulled off my left boot. My first day at jockey school had finally ended, and I was sitting on my bed. I didn't remember ever being so tired and sore in my life.

It was bad enough that I didn't recognize myself in the mirror when I came back to the farm. The girl who looked back at me had straggly hair, broken nails, and a face smeared with dust. Julie and I had seen horror movies where the monster didn't look half as bad.

Even worse, every muscle in my body was screaming for a long, hot bath. When I hadn't been standing, reaching, and bending, I'd been kneeling by a horse to scrape out its hooves with a metal hook. I needed to soak for a good long time to get all the dust and dirt out of my pores and relax my aching muscles.

But I had to get my clothes off first, starting with those awful boots. It's incredible how your toes can swell up after twelve hours in tight-fitting leather. I could have sworn my feet were bigger than the boots.

I yelped again as Christy pulled off the right boot. *"Ouch!"*

"Easy," Christy soothed me. "It's all over. Go and take your bath. You've earned it."

I limped into the bathroom and turned on the water so it ran hard and hot. When I had first come into the house, walking stiffly because I was sure my legs were about to collapse under me, Christy had greeted me with her usual warmth. But when I'd started telling her how tough my first day at Rolling Meadows had been, she'd smiled and changed the subject. It hadn't taken long for me to realize that Christy really didn't want to hear me complaining. Moaning about my day wasn't going to get me any sympathy from her. Either I stuck it out at Rolling Meadows, or I quit.

That was when I really began to miss Julie. Julie would have understood how I felt. I've never been a big complainer, but when I feel like getting something off my chest, Julie has always been around to listen and sympathize. It would have been nice to hear her tell me how strong I was and how much she admired me for not giving up. And there was no way I was going to give up. I'd stick it out, even if it meant seeing Paul Kaufman for only five minutes every day. But I would have liked hearing some encouragement.

Then I remembered that Christy was used to doing farm chores every day. She probably figured that jockey school was a breeze. And obviously she thought it was good for me. My complaining might just make her wish for a niece with a better attitude, and I certainly didn't want that.

I felt a lot better as I washed my hair and let the hot water loosen up my aching muscles. I was so relaxed that I almost dozed off. When the doorbell rang, I hardly heard it.

As I got out of the tub, I heard Christy call my name. "What is it?" I yelled, wrapping myself in a towel.

"Company," she called back. "Come down as soon as you can."

The last thing I felt like was company, but I figured it was probably just some friends of Christy and Harv's. They always introduced me to their friends, and the ones I'd met were pretty nice. I toweled my hair dry and hurried back to my room, where I put on clean shorts, sandals, and an emerald off-the-shoulder shirt that I loved because it made my eyes look even greener than they usually were.

When I got to the living room, I was surprised to see that the "company" was Marla Foster. "Hi," she said in her friendly way. "How was your first day?"

I hesitated and glanced at Christy. I didn't want to say what I really thought in front of her. I knew she didn't want to hear me complain. Luckily Christy took the hint. "Excuse me, Marla. I've got to get dinner ready."

As soon as she left, I blurted out, "I didn't think I was going to live through it!"

Marla laughed. "That's how we all felt at first. You think the day won't ever end, and you'll never be able to stand up straight again as long as you live, and you can't stand the idea of grooming and tacking another horse. Right?"

I felt a surge of relief at her words. At least I wasn't the only person who felt this way! "Exactly," I breathed.

Marla smiled. "Cheer up. It gets easier as you go along. You'll be surprised at how fast you'll get used to it. But listen, I can't stay very long. Everybody's waiting outside."

"Everybody?" I ran to the window, my heart thudding in my chest, and peered at the driveway. A funny-looking old convertible sat there, filled with the other student jockeys. I waved at them, and they all waved back and shouted hello. But I didn't see Paul anywhere among them.

"We're going to the Burger Bandit for dinner," Marla explained. "It's only a couple of miles away, and it's got great food. Want to come with us?"

I thought it sounded like fun. Christy

didn't mind my missing dinner at the farm when Marla explained the outing was a sort of party for all the students. Everybody was laughing and cheerful, and they made room for me when I climbed into the back of the car. All the kids were there—except Paul.

I tried to think of a way to bring up his name without giving away my disappointment that he wasn't there. It wasn't until we were digging into our huge cheeseburgers at Burger Bandit that I finally asked, "Who stays with the horses at night?"

"Nobody," Bobby answered as he devoured a mountain of french fries. "Everybody takes off when the evening feed is over."

"Except Paul." Jo laughed. "You know he spends hours every night on Alfie."

Alfie? I couldn't remember a horse by that name at Rolling Meadows. I must have looked blank, because Greg explained, "Alfie's what we call the bale of hay we practice on when classes are over. We put a saddle on it and hook up the bridle to the stall door, and then we can work for as long as we want. We use Alfie to work on balance, or practice a new handhold, or check our leg position."

I shook my head in disbelief. A bale of hay named Alfie? I must have heard wrong. I never heard of learning to ride by sitting on a bale of hay. *That's crazy,* I told myself. What was even crazier was the idea that Paul was spending his evening with Alfie when he could have been out having fun with a great group of people.

I was dying to know more about Paul but was afraid to ask. Luckily Marla saved me the trouble of asking for details. "Come on, Jo," she said. "You know it's Paul's only free time after all his work is done. If he doesn't practice at night, he won't get enough riding time."

"Enough riding time for *him*," Bobby retorted. "Two hours a day on a horse and another two hours on Alfie is more than enough for *me*."

"He's more dedicated than you are," Wendy said. "He really cares about how well he rides."

Bobby wasn't paying attention. He was looking over my shoulder at something the waitress was bringing to our table. I turned my head and couldn't believe what I saw. It was the biggest chocolate sundae I'd ever seen. Mounds of ice cream, huge froths of whipped cream, and three bright red cherries topped a dish almost as wide as our table. The waitress set the sundae down in front of Bobby, who immediately attacked it with his spoon.

I nudged Marla. "Are we allowed to eat stuff like that?"

Marla grinned. "It's the only way we can keep up our strength after all the veggies and stuff Dutch makes us eat at school. Hey,

Bobby, wait for me!" She grabbed her spoon and thrust it into the sundae. In a minute we were all stuffing ourselves. I decided not to feel guilty about the calories. I'd worked so hard that day that the ice cream probably wouldn't have a chance of settling on my waistline until the end of summer!

By the next day Dutch decided I was a veteran. He told me the "coddling period" was over. "What coddling period?" I asked. "You mean I was being *coddled* yesterday?"

He pretended to swat me. "Get over there and get some cold-water wraps ready. We'll be using a lot of them today."

I went over to the barrel where the wraps were kept. It was filled with water, and I found out exactly how cold the wraps were the minute I plunged my hands in. Even though it was warm outside, my hands turned to ice at once. In a few seconds my fingers were so stiff, I could hardly shape them around the cloths to roll them the way Paul had shown me.

Each long, narrow cloth had to be rolled up tightly. Then, when the horses were ready to be exercised, someone always wrapped cold-waters around each of their legs. The wraps protected them from injuries during the morning workouts.

I knew the wraps were important, but so were my frozen hands. I pulled them out of the water and hunted for something to wipe them on. If I could just get my circulation going again, I was sure I could handle the rest of the wraps in no time.

"Here you go!" A warm, dry cloth hit me right in the face. When I pulled it off, I saw Paul grinning at me.

"Just what I needed," I told him, wrapping the cloth around my aching fingers. "Thanks a lot."

"You're welcome. It looked like your fingers were about to freeze solid."

"I thought they were." I laughed. I couldn't believe how easy it suddenly was to talk to Paul. Even as we were laughing together, though, I could feel my heart fluttering under my T-shirt. Maybe he wasn't the big, muscular boy of my dreams, but this guy did something to my insides, and I hoped it would never stop!

"Enough socializing, folks," came Dutch's voice. "We've got work to do and horses to look after here. Keep your minds on your jobs."

Paul nodded to indicate to Dutch that he'd heard, but he turned back to give me some reassurance. "Easy does it," he advised. "Dutch doesn't mean you have to slave every minute. You're pulling your weight all right."

I glanced at Dutch, who was walking away toward the office. "Do you think he knows that?"

"*I* know it," Paul answered, and the smile he gave me made me glow all over. It was funny. At school I wanted the guys to think I was the happy-go-lucky type. Here, where everybody worked so hard, I wanted to be taken seriously. Paul's approval made me feel terrific. At the same time, it surprised me. I'd been at jockey school for less than two days, yet already I could feel my attitude beginning to change. Before, I had picked my friends based on some pretty superficial qualities. I liked people who were well-dressed and popular and fun to be around. If the girls I met liked parties and shopping and talking about guys, we usually hit it off.

Now I found myself becoming interested in other kinds of people, both girls and guys. Since the conversation at the Burger Bandit the night before, I'd begun to appreciate kids who were focused and ambitious, particularly guys who worked longer, harder hours than other people because they loved what they did and wanted to be the best they could be. Particularly Paul.

As I started to roll the wraps again in the freezing water, I smiled to myself. Mom and Dad would probably applaud if they could see me now!

Chapter Four

On Saturday morning I waited nervously by one of the vacant stalls for Dutch to come out of the main house. All the kids who passed by gave me a thumbs-up and some encouraging words. I needed them. There were huge butterflies churning around in my stomach.

I'd spent the last five days at Rolling Meadows learning barn procedure, which was the first step in jockey training. I wasn't even allowed to get on a horse until I passed three tests. Today I planned to take two of them.

The first test was mucking out a stall properly. Ever since Paul had shown me how to do it, I'd practiced hard. I knew how to rake the shavings inside the stall into a neat square and sift through all the hay and straw for horse droppings. The problem was, I had to do the whole stall in a half hour to pass the test. That included dumping the horse droppings at the refuse heap and gathering new shavings to finish off the stall.

When Dutch was satisfied with that, I'd have to groom and tack a horse properly, again in a half hour. I'd worked on that, too. Marla and Jo had coached me and shown me how to brush, sponge, and curry the horse and put on the saddle, padding, race cloth, and bridle. It could be tricky if you didn't know what you were doing. I just hoped I did. After watching everyone working so hard all week, I was determined to match their progress. By the end of the summer, I wanted to be a first-class rider.

"All set?" Dutch asked as he strolled into the stable area. We were alone; everyone else had their assignments for the morning and was already at work. I could hear Paul calling instructions to the others.

I swallowed hard. "I think so."

Dutch raised an eyebrow at me, as if he weren't sure I was ready. But all he said was, "Okay, then. Half an hour. Let's go."

I glanced at my watch and plunged into the stall. I'd set out the wheelbarrow and rake exactly where I wanted them, in the center of the stall, and in a minute I was raking furiously. I worked my way down the first side of the stall, conscious that the clock was ticking and Dutch was standing outside, watching me closely. I knew he wouldn't grade me on the way I worked, just on the final condition of the stall, so I didn't really mind his looking over my shoulder. I was just determined to be done in record time!

Either it was a very messy stall to begin with, or my zeal for the job was uncovering more than the usual amount of droppings. In any case the wheelbarrow was full in just a few minutes. I raced out to dump it and raced back, this time attacking the center of the stall.

Dutch looked casually at his watch, which made me even more frantic. I glanced at my own watch and saw that I had about twelve minutes left. I gathered all the old shavings in the middle of the stall, as Paul had taught me to do, and made a neat line around the edge of it. Now all I had to do was get fresh shavings from the pile behind the stables.

Once more I dashed out with the wheelbarrow. I scooped up the shavings as fast as I could, tossed them into the wheelbarrow, and rushed back toward the stall. I was moving so fast, I saw only a blur before I collided with something right in my path.

"Ouch!" a voice cried.

I'd hit one of the other students! I looked up, ready to apologize, and saw Paul sprawled in the dust. What was worse, he had been holding the hose, and when he fell, he dropped it, spraying water all over my lovely fresh shavings and me. In a few seconds I was soaked to the skin, and the shavings were ruined.

"Oh, no! My stall!" I wailed.

"Your stall? What about my leg?" Paul demanded, clutching his knee and rolling around in pain. "And my hose!" He made a grab for it and turned it away from the wheelbarrow. I looked down at my watch again. I had about six minutes left. In those six minutes I had to dump the wet shavings, scoop up fresh ones, get them to my stall, and spread them out properly before Dutch's inspection!

But Paul was obviously hurt, and I couldn't just leave him lying there. "I'm awfully sorry," I told him. "Are you all right?"

He rubbed at the sore spot below his knee. "Well, I think I'll live," he said wryly. "I may limp for a few years, but there's no permanent damage."

"Can I help you?" I wanted to reach out and help him to his feet, but when his great brown eyes suddenly narrowed, I thought better of it. It was probably smarter to leave him alone. Maybe he was mad at me for bumping into him, though it really had been an accident. Could I convince him of that?

I stood there helplessly as he stared at me. Then he said, "You're taking the test now, aren't you?"

I nodded.

"How much time do you have left?"

I fumbled at my watch. "About five—maybe four and a half minutes, I think."

"Well, then, get going!" he exclaimed. "Come on, get fresh shavings! *Move!*"

For a moment I just stared at him. I'd run the guy down with a wheelbarrow. He was still in pain, but all he could think about was my finishing the test, as if it were a matter of life and death!

"Go on, Barrie! I don't want you to fail because of me. Go on, hurry!"

It seemed a little crazy to me. I was used to doing my best and accepting it if someone else did better. Yet here was Paul, urging me on to a new level of competition, acting as if mucking out a stall were the most important thing in the world! What had I gotten myself into?

Before I let myself think about that, I took Paul's advice. I dashed back to the shavings pile, loaded up my wheelbarrow again, and charged back to the stall—this time keeping an eye peeled for pedestrians. I had only one minute left when I tipped the wheelbarrow over in the stall and dumped out the new shavings.

I set to work with the rake as fast as I could, smoothing the new shavings over the old. The rest of the stall looked picture perfect. I hoped Dutch wouldn't take away too many points if the shavings weren't spread out properly when the time was up.

When I heard Dutch call "Time!" I stopped and stepped outside the stall. As he walked in, I tried to read his expression, but it was impossible. Slowly he surveyed the stall, kicking at patches of the shavings for stray droppings. He inspected the indentation I'd made all around the stall with the rake. Then he came out. I could hardly breathe as I waited for his verdict.

Dutch nodded. "Not bad."

I stared at him. "I passed?"

"Yep, you passed," he said calmly. I wondered if he could hear my heart hammering against my ribs. "Want to rest a little before you take the grooming and tacking test? Or maybe change your shirt?" Dutch added with a twinkle in his eye as he looked inquiringly at my damp T-shirt. It felt really uncomfortable. I'd rather be in a wet bathing suit than a wet T-shirt any day.

Of course, since I was living with Christy and Harv, I didn't keep a change of clothes in the dorm. I wouldn't be able to run to the farm and change and come back in less than half an hour. But the sun was shining, and I figured I'd be dry in no time. I shrugged and grinned at Dutch. "Nah. I'm on a roll. Let's get it over with!"

Wendy, Jo, Tessa, and Marla were thrilled when I told them a while later that I passed both my barn tests. After lunch they brought me a cupcake with a candle in it, and everybody sang a chorus of "For She's a Jolly Good Fellow." I was really touched that they cared so much about how I did. It felt as if we were all a little family, with everybody rooting for everybody else.

Later that afternoon Bobby gave me my first lesson on Alfie. I quickly discovered that Alfie wasn't just a bale of hay like the ones in the loft above the stables. He was a *huge* bale of hay, the height and breadth of a very large horse. I had a hard time scrambling into the saddle, and when I was seated, I was too tired from my full day's work to pay much attention to what Bobby was teaching me.

"Feet in the irons, like this," he instructed, turning my toes inward and pulling my heels down. "And move your legs a little more forward. Hands down."

I tried to do what I was told, but all the muscles in my arms and legs were trembling with exhaustion. I knew it was hopeless. I didn't have any energy left. "Look, Bobby," I said, "I really appreciate your help, but I just can't do any more today."

"Copping out, huh?" Bobby commented. I'd already noticed that while he was always delighted to take a break or lead the group to the Burger Bandit, Bobby was also the first to criticize someone else for sloppy work habits or laziness. He was the only one of the group who made remarks about other students' abilities, and I didn't like him as much as I liked the others.

"I'm not copping out," I tried to explain. "I just can't concentrate anymore. I took my barn tests today, and I put in a full day's work besides. I think I'd better just rest for a while and start fresh on Monday."

Bobby shrugged. "Whatever. It doesn't matter to me if you're not ready to be an exercise rider by the end of the summer."

"Hey, that's not fair!" I was angry. "I just started here this week. I've been learning all these new things and trying to keep up with the rest of you while I do them. I've listened and paid attention and done my share of the work. There's no reason to pick on me just because I haven't got any energy left!"

"What's going on?" Paul asked, walking into the empty stall where Alfie was rigged up.

"Nothing. See you at the picnic." Bobby pushed past him and left the stall without another glance at me. I sat on top of Alfie, still fuming.

"Planning on being up there all night?" Paul asked pleasantly.

I slid my feet out of the stirrups and slid off Alfie's saddle. "I'm done," I said. "You want to put in some time?"

Paul nodded. "I usually do when my work's finished."

I wondered if that meant he wouldn't be at

the jockeys' picnic. Tired as I was, I was looking forward to it. I'd planned to change into something really pretty and feminine—something completely different from my jeans and Rolling Meadows T-shirt—to show Paul I could actually look decent once in a while. I hoped that if he saw me looking nice, he'd respond with more than his usual friendliness.

"Aren't you coming to the picnic?" I asked. "It sounds like fun. I hear they've been planning it for two weeks."

"I'll drop by when I'm done here." He set down a large portable cassette player in the corner of the stall and slipped in a tape.

"Hey, that's a good idea," I said enthusiastically. "When you listen to music while you're working, it really makes the time fly by."

Paul smiled mysteriously. "It's not music on that tape."

"Then what is it?"

I could swear I actually saw Paul Kaufman blushing. For a minute he didn't answer.

"Paul, what is it?"

Finally he said, "You won't tell the others? They'll probably think I'm nuts."

He was trusting me with a secret! He thought enough of me to let me share something the other kids didn't know about! I was so thrilled, I could hardly get the words out. "I won't tell a soul. I promise."

He hesitated for a moment more. Then he said, "Okay. Give me a leg up." He stood by

Alfie, one leg curled behind him. I had seen the others boosting each other into the saddle, but I hadn't ever tried it. I hoped I wouldn't embarrass myself by messing it up.

But Paul wasn't very heavy. He lifted easily into the saddle and adjusted the stirrup leathers expertly. He made a swift knot in the reins, set his heels down firmly, and nodded to me. "Okay. Hit the Play button."

I couldn't imagine what I was going to hear, but I loved the fact that whatever it was, it was strictly between Paul and me. I pushed the button and waited. Paul tensed in the saddle.

A professional-sounding voice came on, announcing a race for four-year-olds at the Fountain, the biggest racetrack nearby. "The horses are approaching the starting gate," the announcer intoned.

Paul saw my bewilderment. "I taped this from TV," he explained. "This one ran about three weeks ago. Listen."

"Aaannd—*they're off!*" The announcer began to describe the action of the horses running the race. I turned to see Paul's reaction and found him just as involved in the race as if he were riding in it himself!

He sat on top of Alfie, reins in both hands, leaning forward in a rhythmic pattern that would be perfect on a racehorse straining toward the finish line. As the announcer's voice grew taut with excitement, Paul reached into his pocket for his whip, which he banged against both sides of the hay bale as though he were urging on a real horse.

As the race neared the end, Paul seemed to forget I was there. He was peering over his shoulder at imaginary competitors behind him, urging on his straw "horse" with his hands and legs. "And—it's—Charge Account by a length, followed by Wire Frames and Flipperwill!" The announcer's voice died away.

Paul sat back on Alfie and motioned to me to turn off the tape. Now that the "race" was over, he seemed to realize that he was sitting on a bale of hay in a dim, quiet stall with a girl he didn't know very well, and a tape recorder. I saw a flush come over his cheeks. Obviously he was afraid I was going to make fun of him.

Nothing was further from my mind. I'd gotten all caught up in the excitement of the race, and I wasn't at all tired anymore. In fact, I'd even cheered Paul on to victory!

"Paul, that was *great!*" I told him as he jumped down and stood beside me. "I've never been this close to a winning jockey before."

The embarrassed look on Paul's face gave way to his usual sunny smile. "You should see me on a good day," he joked. "I ride nine winners a day, weather permitting."

We both laughed, but I couldn't help remembering that instant when he had looked so vulnerable, as though I could really hurt him with a thoughtless remark. And there was something about the way he was looking at me now that made me tingle all over.

Abruptly Paul broke the mood. "Listen, Barrie, don't you want to go to that picnic? If you don't hurry up, you'll probably miss some really good burgers and salads."

But I wasn't about to leave if he wasn't. "What about you? Are you going to work some more?"

"Why?"

Suddenly I just had to say what popped into my head. "Because if you're not, I could use some more help on Alfie. Bobby tried to teach me, but I don't really have a clue about what I'm supposed to be doing."

Paul looked at me. Somehow it was different from all the times he'd looked at me before. It was as if, for the first time, he was taking me seriously. "Won't you mind missing the picnic?" he asked softly.

I shook my head, gazing right into his beautiful brown eyes. "No. I think what I'm doing here is a lot more important."

Chapter Five

"Keep your heels down," Paul said a moment later. He had boosted me into Alfie's saddle and was checking my position. "Why don't you try posting a little?"

I wasn't very good at posting, but I knew it was important for jockeys to learn. I pretended that Alfie was a real horse, just as Paul had done, and imagined he was trotting. I began to raise myself in the stirrups in a rhythmic pattern: stand one beat, sit one beat, over and over again. Soon my legs started to ache.

"That's good," Paul approved, walking around to face me. "How does it feel?"

"Boring." I grinned down at him. "Is this all there is to it?"

"You could whistle or something if you want to keep busy," Paul teased. "Anyway, you'd better get used to it. Remember, you can't ride the school horses until you pass your Alfie test, and in the Alfie test you'll have to post for fifteen minutes without stopping."

"Fifteen minutes?" I hadn't thought it would be that long.

"Think you can handle it?"

I recovered quickly. I wasn't going to let him think I couldn't do it! "Uh, sure. No problem."

"It's not really that bad," he assured me. "You'd be surprised how fast the time goes when you're talking to someone."

It sure does, I thought. I forgot all about my aches and pains when Paul began to show me the correct leg positions. He was a good teacher, strict but very encouraging. It surprised me that I was actually concentrating on what I was doing. Usually in school I spent a lot of time daydreaming about what I'd be doing after class. But right now there was no place I would rather be.

"I guess I should show you how to throw crosses," Paul said after a while, gazing up at me. My heart began to beat faster as I saw the way he was looking at me—not like a teacher, but like the hopeful boy who'd ridden a straw "winner" past the finish line in an imaginary race. I loved seeing him that way.

"What's throwing crosses?" I asked, but I couldn't have cared less about the answer.

Our eyes locked, and without a word I kicked my feet out of the stirrups and slid to the ground. I wanted to keep looking into his eyes, but my legs were turning to jelly under me, and I suddenly felt shy. So I busied myself unbuckling the girth of the saddle.

All of a sudden I felt Paul's hands on my neck and shoulders, massaging my aching muscles as though he knew exactly where they hurt. I was too thrilled to speak. His hands felt so warm and gentle. Everything else was blurry around me. All I could focus on was the touch of his hands. His fingertips moved lightly up my neck to my scalp, and I tilted my head forward. I couldn't believe anything could feel so good.

"Barrie?" Paul's voice was husky behind me, and I slowly turned around. I was sure he was going to kiss me, and I knew it was going to be wonderful. I raised my head and gazed deep into those gorgeous brown eyes. . . .

"Currr-few!" roared a voice practically in my ear. Paul and I jumped at the sound. Dutch was standing in the doorway, grinning at us and pointing to his watch. "Nine o'clock, kids. Barrie, you did a good day's work. Now you can either join the others at the picnic or get on home. You, too, Paul. No more work tonight. That's an order."

For a minute I was bewildered at the sudden transition from magical romance to everyday reality. Then I was furious. What was

Dutch doing sneaking around in the stables after dark? Why wasn't he at the picnic?

I hoped that now he'd made his announcement, he'd at least go away and let me say good night to Paul alone. But Dutch waited as I gathered up Alfie's saddle and bridle. *He's doing this on purpose!* I raged inwardly. *He knows we want to be alone.*

Paul obviously realized it, too. "Dutch, we weren't quite finished—" he started, but Dutch cut him off.

"For Pete's sake, boy, you know the rules. Nine o'clock is lights out on all stable work. If you haven't got it done by then, do it in the morning. Sometimes you just plain work too hard." He waved away Paul's protests. "Last thing I need on the place is *two* workaholics."

"Workaholic?" my mother repeated when I phoned home the next day. "Mr. Callahan thinks *you're* becoming a workaholic?"

"Believe it or not, Mom, I really am working hard," I told her. "And I'm having a great time!"

"Well, I'm glad of that, honey," Mom said a little doubtfully. "You're taking care of yourself, aren't you?"

"I really am," I assured her. "And Christy and Harv are taking good care of me, too. Good food, lots of exercise, sunshine, and I get to bed at a decent hour every night."

"You sound tired," Mom insisted.

Trust a mother to know when something's wrong. I wasn't tired, but I was discouraged. I hadn't heard a word from Paul since our work on Alfie the night before. I was wondering whether he had forgotten all about what had almost happened between us. I'd been hoping he might call just to say hello, but so far he hadn't. Since it was Sunday, and classes at Rolling Meadows wouldn't resume until Monday, I wouldn't see Paul until then.

Christy saw the look on my face when I hung up the phone. "No word from him, huh?"

I shook my head. I must have looked as glum as I felt, because Christy reached out to hug me. "Cheer up, Barrie. I've never seen you look like this. You've always been such an 'up' person."

"I used to be," I said gloomily.

"What do you do at home when you feel like this?" Christy asked.

I couldn't help grinning. "Go shopping at the mall. Any place around here where I could do some damage?"

Christy laughed. "Nothing like what you're used to, I'm afraid. We'd have to drive to Greenwich or Stamford to make the kind of dent you're talking about."

"How about another kind of picker-upper?" Harv suggested.

"Like what?" I asked.

"Like a swimming party next Sunday here at our lake? You could invite all the kids from school, barbecue some hot dogs and chicken, make a day of it. What do you think?"

I thought it was inspired. "That sounds *super!*" I ran over to my uncle and gave him a big hug. "I'd love a swimming party, and I'll bet everyone else will love it, too!"

"Including Paul?" Christy asked archly.

"Especially Paul—even if I have to drag him here myself!" I laughed.

I was right. Everyone did love the idea of the swimming party when I told them about it on Monday morning. Even Dutch agreed to come. I didn't make a big deal of it to Paul, who said he'd try to make it. But he didn't seem very enthusiastic, and I knew something was wrong. To keep my mind occupied, I concentrated on my work at school. I wanted to take my Alfie test by midweek and start riding real horses as soon as I could.

I wasn't worried about the fifteen minutes of posting. I'd been practicing and practicing, though Paul didn't coach me again, and I knew I could post for that long without tiring. What bothered me was the second part of the test. After the posting someone would grab the bridle and pretend that my "horse" was running away. He or she would tug as hard as possible, trying to make me lose my balance and drop the reins. I had to hold out, using all my strength, for five solid minutes.

"You'll be fine," Marla told me confidently as we walked toward Alfie's stall after chores on Wednesday. "I've been watching you work. Next to Paul I'd say you're the hardest-working person around here. There's no way you won't make it."

I was glad to hear her words, though I knew it was still very possible I would fail. I *had* been working hard the last few days, and it was paying off. My arms and legs were already a lot stronger. Between the barn work and the Alfie exercises, my body was in better shape than it had ever been before.

Unfortunately, my relationship with Paul wasn't. I had hardly seen him since Saturday night. When we did pass each other in the stable yard, he acted as though I weren't even there. I didn't get it. What was the matter? He was never actually rude to me, but he didn't tease me or talk to me and certainly didn't share any more secrets with me.

I began to feel awkward around him, especially since I didn't think there was anything I needed to apologize for or be ashamed of. I tried to guess why he was acting so cold. Was he upset that Dutch had caught us almost kissing? Were the others talking about it behind our backs and teasing him? I didn't know. I just knew that jockey school had been a lot of fun last week, and now it wasn't.

But I was determined to prove to Paul that whether he cared about me or not, I was going to be a world-class exercise rider. Besides, it helped take my mind off my misery when I spent an extra hour or two on Alfie night after night. Paul didn't seem to be working with Alfie at all anymore, or if he did, it was after I left. At home I might have gone on an all-out shopping spree to drown my sorrows, but at Rolling Meadows there was nothing to do but ride. So that's what I did, even if the horse in question was only a bale of hay. Wendy and Jo worked with me on posting, coaching me for the Alfie test.

"Hey, Dutch!" Marla yelled as we got to Alfie's stall. "She's all set!"

Dutch came out of the feed room and frowned. "You sure, Barrie? You want to try it now?"

"I'm sure," I said as I fastened the strap on my new regulation hard hat. "I think I can pass."

Dutch shrugged. "Okay, but you're moving awfully fast. Still, if that's what you want—" He scanned the yard for a moment. "Bobby, you free? Nah—you take care of Satin Girl, that's okay. Where's Paul?"

Oh, no! Don't make me take the test in front of Paul! I cried inwardly. I could feel my face turning bright red as Paul came over to

Dutch, his eyes deliberately averted from me. He was wiping his hands with a clean cloth, and I couldn't help noticing how nice he looked in his jeans and white T-shirt.

"Time Barrie on the Alfie test, will you?" Dutch said casually. "I'll be in the ring with the school horses."

"Sure," Paul said, still avoiding my gaze. "Let's go." He walked into the stall without even looking to see if I was following him.

"Good luck," Marla called as she hurried after Dutch.

I saddled and bridled Alfie in silence. Paul didn't say one word either, and I couldn't think of any way to say what was on my mind. *Concentrate on the test,* I told myself. *You want to learn how to be an exercise rider, so think about what you're learning. Forget about Paul. He's obviously got a split personality.*

"All set?" Paul asked after I tested the girth to be sure it was tight enough. I nodded. "Okay, then. Belly up."

At my height, it hadn't been easy for me to learn how to throw myself over the saddle and lift myself into a sitting position. My head was barely level with Alfie's back. During the test I wasn't allowed to ask for a leg up. Jumping high enough to get myself into the saddle had taken long hours of practice. I only hoped I wouldn't do something really stupid now that Paul was watching.

Fortunately, I made it on the first try and easily got my feet into the irons. Although my hands were trembling, I braided the reins into an exercise rider's knot and settled myself in the saddle. "I'm ready," I told Paul.

He nodded and glanced at his watch. "Post for fifteen minutes, starting . . . *now*." Not looking at him, I started to raise and lower myself in the saddle, once again imagining that Alfie was a real horse. In a minute I'd established the right rhythm. It was just a matter of keeping it up for fifteen minutes. I'd done it before, and I knew I could do it this time.

What I hadn't counted on was the silence. Whenever I'd worked on this part of the test with Jo and Wendy, we'd been laughing and talking. Paul had been right. Time went fast when you had someone to talk to while you worked. Now, though, there was no conversation at all. Paul watched me silently, looking at his watch once in a while. I bounced up and down in the saddle, feeling more and more uncomfortable. If only he would say something!

Finally, I couldn't take it anymore. "Cat got your tongue?" I inquired between bounces.

Paul smiled faintly but said nothing.

"How much longer? I asked. Actually, it didn't really matter. Now that I'd caught the rhythm, I figured I could post for half a day if I had to. It was the quiet I couldn't take much more of.

Paul checked his watch again. "About six and a half minutes. Getting tired?"

"No," I said. "But I *am* a little curious." When he still said nothing, I persisted. "You want to explain to me why we had such a good time last Saturday night, and you aren't even speaking to me this week? Has something happened that I don't know about? Or are you sorry that you let me in on your secret?"

Paul flushed. "Of course not. Why, did it bother you?"

"Of course not," I said. "I thought it was great. I think it makes work so much more exciting when you keep your mind on your goal like that. And I was flattered that you were willing to share it with me."

I hadn't stopped posting while I said all this, but I could see Paul's expression softening. The tight, closed look he'd worn for days began to fade away. When he glanced at me again, I got a glimpse of the sensitive, gentle boy I'd seen Saturday night. A thrill jolted through me and made me bold enough to demand, "So why have you ignored me all week?"

For a moment I thought Paul was going to blurt out whatever it was. Instead, he said quietly, "Time's up. Get ready to be pulled."

I took a deep breath and closed my hands more firmly on the reins. "I'm all set."

"Okay." He yanked the front of the bridle so hard, I thought my shoulders would rip out of their sockets. I pulled back, hanging on with every ounce of strength I had. Paul obviously wasn't going to make this part of the test easy for me. He was doing a good job of acting like a runaway horse galloping out of control. I was determined to act like a professional rider and stop him in his tracks.

"You haven't answered my question," I panted between clenched teeth, hanging on to the bridle with everything I had. I could feel the sweat beginning to drip down my face from under my helmet. "Why haven't you been talking to me?"

Paul tightened his fingers on the bridle and pulled with all his might. "It's nothing personal."

"Sure it is," I panted. "If it had nothing to do with me . . . you'd have at least been polite. You've been acting like . . . I don't even exist. Why?"

"Can't this wait?" Paul asked. He was beginning to pant, too.

"No, it can't wait! Why . . . won't you . . . talk to me . . . the way you . . . did?"

Paul stopped pulling and looked up at me. "Look, I have a job to do here! I'm not a student who pays tuition. I'm Dutch's stable assistant. He pays me a salary to do my job. I have to practice riding on my own time."

"So?" I was beginning to feel a little faint. It was pretty hot in the stall, and my helmet felt heavy. My fingers were burning from gripping the leather reins. My legs were aching from clutching Alfie's sides as tightly as possible. Every muscle in my body was exhausted.

"So . . ." Paul adjusted his position and yanked again. "So I can't afford to socialize the way the other kids do. I haven't got time, if I'm going to make myself into a good jockey. I have to concentrate on my work."

"And being friends with me would interfere with that?" I demanded as I held on.

Paul braced his feet against Alfie, pulling even harder. "It already has," he said grimly. "I've been thinking about you when I should be concentrating on my riding. Instead of keeping my mind on my job, I've been wondering whether you'd go out with me after classes are over. I don't like it!" He looked at his watch. "Thirty seconds to go. At twenty seconds I'm really going to pull hard. Ready?"

"Am I ever!" I cried. I was so happy, I almost laughed. Paul didn't hate me! In fact, he liked me so much that he was thinking about me instead of his job, which apparently had never happened before. Knowing that, I felt strong enough to hold onto twenty runaway horses!

The last ten seconds of the test were torture on my body, but my heart was lighter than it had been in days. Everything was going to be all right. I was sure I could find a way to show Paul that I could help, not hurt, his career. And I had the rest of the summer to prove it.

"You passed!" Paul shouted exultantly as time ran out. "Nice job!" He dropped the bridle and reached out to take my hand. "How do you feel?"

I had at least two enormous blisters on each hand. My arms were trembling with fatigue, and my legs were throbbing with the worst cramps I'd ever had. My whole body was drenched in sweat, and I could feel my wet hair sticking to my scalp under the helmet.

I smiled radiantly at him. "I never felt better in my life!"

Chapter Six

"Four, five, six bags of potato chips," Christy counted on Sunday morning. "You think that's enough?"

I laughed. "Christy, there's only going to be about a dozen of us. That's two people per bag. It's *more* than enough."

Harv looked over the food spread out on the picnic table in the backyard. "Hey, ladies, what's all this? Is Dutch bringing over his horses today, too? I thought it was just a bunch of short kids with big appetites!"

"Stop teasing, Harv." Christy began to slice carrots. "I just don't want anybody to go home hungry."

Harv and I exchanged smiles. Christy might often look and act like one of my girlfriends, but when it came to entertaining, she was just like my mother. Everybody had to be stuffed to the gills for Christy to be satisfied that she was a good hostess.

I was pretty impressed myself when I took a good look at the feast. There were big bowls of potato salad and cole slaw, trays of hot dogs and chicken ready for the barbecue, and a platter of celery sticks, carrots, radishes, and tomatoes surrounding Christy's special dip. I had fixed pitchers of lemonade and iced tea for anyone who didn't want cold soda. It looked as if there were enough to feed the entire town of Wellspring.

The guests started arriving before noon. I led them to the lake behind the farmhouse, where we would be having our picnic.

"Wahoo! What a great spot!" Greg threw himself into one of the lounge chairs Harv had placed under the shade of some weeping-willow trees. "Fantastic!"

"Fantastic is right," Wendy agreed. She tossed off her white cotton cover-up to reveal a neon pink bathing suit so bright it probably glowed in the dark. My sleek black tank suit looked pretty drab in comparison. Marla, Jo, and Tessa soon followed Wendy's example, and when Bobby and Dutch arrived, everyone plunged into the crystal-clear water. Even Dutch went in for a quick dip.

Christy came up next to me as I watched the others swim. "He's not here yet, is he?" she asked softly.

I shook my head. "He said he'd come. Maybe he just got busy with something." As far as I was concerned, the party wouldn't really start until Paul arrived.

Christy gave me an encouraging hug. "He'll make it."

And he did. When I came out of the house a few minutes later with more chips and dip, Paul was there, looking even more terrific than usual in dark blue swim trunks and a Rolling Meadows T-shirt. "Hi, Barrie," he said with a grin. "Have you been in yet?"

"Not yet," I said, feeling my spirits lift. "I was waiting for you. Want to try it?"

Paul glanced over at the lake. Everyone was yelling and dunking each other. "Not right now," he said. "I think I'd rather hang out with the hostess and just talk for a while. Unless there's something I can do to help?"

Christy had been refilling some platters a few feet away, and she heard his last remark. The look she shot me said, *I like this guy.*

"Not right now," I told Paul. "But stick around. Something's sure to come up. In the meantime let me introduce you to my aunt and uncle, Christy and Harv Allison."

After the introductions had been made, the four of us stood around talking for a while. Almost before I knew it, it was time for lunch.

When everyone had eaten as much as he or she could, they lazed around on the grass, talking about horses and racing. Beneath the willows I could hear Dutch trying to persuade

Christy and Harv to let him train Plum Rose at Rolling Meadows. "She's gonna be something," he kept saying. "Why won't you let her race?"

"Don't you have enough going on over there without another horse?" Harv asked him.

"As much as I can handle." Dutch laughed. "In fact, there may even be some new students coming in. Frankly, I don't know if I'll have a place to put them in the dormitories."

"Why not send them over here?" Christy suggested. "We've got plenty of extra room, and your students would be company for Barrie."

I didn't have time to listen to the rest of the conversation. I was busy bringing out more charcoal and sodas, and Paul was helping me. "Don't you want to sit down and relax with everyone else?" I asked him once. I didn't want him giving me a hand if he was doing it just to be polite.

"I don't like crowds much," he answered. "Besides, I'm happy where I am."

That made me happy, too. Still, I felt I had to object. "You might be missing something really fun," I said. "I think they're going to have a tug-of-war in a few minutes."

Paul smiled at me. "Do you really want to do that?"

If I'd been at home, I probably would have said yes. I always liked being part of a big, noisy group. Since I'd met Paul, though, I was beginning to realize that groups weren't necessarily the most fun. I could have just as much fun with one person, if it was the right person. And Paul was definitely the right person!

Instead of joining the others for the tug-of-war, Paul and I wandered off together and found a spot hidden by the trees that ringed the lake. We could hear the others, but we couldn't see them, and they couldn't see us. The trees and grass smelled summer fresh. It was a wonderful spot for a quiet talk.

I flopped down on the grass, and Paul settled himself against the trunk of a weeping willow. We didn't say anything for a while. We just sat, looking at each other. I realized then that I had never seen him away from Rolling Meadows. This was the very first time we'd been together without being surrounded by horses! The thought made me giggle.

"Are you laughing at me?" he asked with a smile.

"No. It's just funny. . . ." It took me a minute to get myself under control. "You know, I don't even know what you do when you're not at Rolling Meadows. I mean, what you like to do aside from jockey training." Then I had a horrible thought. What if that was all he liked to do? What if he wasn't interested in anything but horses?

"What do *you* like to do?" Paul asked,

neatly reversing the question. "You don't live just to be an exercise rider, do you?"

"Oh, no." I laughed again. "I like to do lots of things."

"Like what?"

"Like . . . dancing. Shopping. Movies."

"What kind of movies do you like?" Paul sounded genuinely interested. He was still leaning against the tree, but it seemed as if the distance between us were suddenly a lot smaller.

"Different kinds." My throat felt dry, and I wished I'd brought along some lemonade. "Mostly I love big action movies like *Top Gun* and a lot of the comic-book stuff. I saw *Batman* three times and *Dick Tracy* five."

"I like the action stuff, too," Paul agreed. He got up and moved closer to me, sitting beside me on the grassy bank. "But I like some serious stuff just as much. I thought *The Untouchables* was great. Did you see that?"

I remembered seeing it on video and liking it very much. Another thing I liked very much was the fact that he was next to me. "Yes. It was really good. I'd forgotten about that."

"I like just about anything Kevin Costner does," Paul went on enthusiastically. "I have tapes of *Bull Durham* and *Field of Dreams*, and for my birthday last year, my older brother got me a copy of *Silverado*."

They were some of my favorite movies, too. I was thrilled that Paul and I liked the same things. It made me feel more comfortable with him. "So if Costner does a racing movie, you'll be first in line to see it, right?" I asked.

Paul looked into my eyes. "That's right." He reached over and gently brushed my hair away from my face. My heartbeat quickened.

"Well, well. What have we here?" Bobby pushed aside the long trailing strands of weeping willow and stomped into our little clearing. "No wonder we didn't have a full team for the tug-of-war!"

I blushed, but Paul just eyed Bobby calmly. "What's the matter? Can't you guys have a good time without us?"

"Well, you're obviously having a good time without *us*," Bobby said with a knowing grin.

The romantic moment was over—again. First Dutch had spoiled the mood that night in Alfie's stall. Now Bobby had cut short our first real conversation that didn't center on racing. As Paul, Bobby, and I went back to join the others, I wondered whether we'd *ever* get some uninterrupted time alone.

Apparently, Paul wondered the same thing. As the rest of the kids were thanking Christy and Harv and starting back toward Rolling Meadows, he hung back. "This is getting ridiculous," he told me. "It seems like we never get a chance to really talk."

I nodded, my heart hammering. With an opening like that, surely he was going to ask me out. I cast about for something else to say. "I know what you mean. If it isn't the horses, it's Dutch or one of the other students."

"You said it! Maybe we should try to talk somewhere away from all of them."

"Like where?" I asked, thinking, *Please, please, let him ask me out!*

"Do you like ice cream?" Paul asked. "There's a great little place in town called The Topping. It's an old-fashioned soda fountain. A lot of the kids who live around here hang out there."

"That sounds like fun," I replied enthusiastically. I couldn't believe my luck. I'd have two of my favorite things, a hot-fudge sundae and Paul Kaufman, together in one evening!

"How about tomorrow night, after supper? Seven o'clock okay?"

"You mean we'd have to abandon Alfie?" I teased.

"What the heck. Let's live a little." Paul grinned at me.

"You're on," I told him. He didn't say another word, but as he walked away to join the others, I could still see his warm smile in my mind's eye.

"He's terrific," Christy told me later that evening as we scraped the leftover food into bowls and covered them with plastic wrap. "The nicest one of the whole bunch."

"And a good worker, too," Harv added, putting the leftovers in the fridge. "Dutch says he puts in longer hours than anybody there. He thinks Paul will turn into a top-notch jockey if he keeps at it."

"He asked me out tomorrow night after school," I confided. "We're going to The Topping." I was so happy, I felt as if I were going to burst.

Christy was just as thrilled as I was. "Barrie, that's great! What are you going to wear?"

I thought about the clothes situation. There wasn't much to work with. I hadn't *really* expected to meet my gorgeous guy while I was visiting my aunt and uncle. All I'd brought were a couple of light cotton dresses and a few skirts and blouses. "What's The Topping like?" I asked. "Is it real casual? Paul said it's an ice-cream parlor."

Christy thought for a moment. "Yes, it is, but there's dancing, too. I've seen kids wearing some pretty hot stuff there. Tell you what. Let's go up to your room and check out your wardrobe."

So we did. When I opened my closet door, Christy fingered one of my dresses, a pale mint green with a full skirt and a scoop neckline. "How about this?"

I shrugged. "It's nothing special, though.

What would I wear with it? I didn't bring any accessories."

Christy smiled mysteriously and left the room. When she came back a moment later, she was holding a gorgeous silvery scarf.

"Oh, Christy, that's fabulous!"

"Tie it around your waist," she suggested. As soon as I did, I knew it was the perfect accent to the outfit. Then I remembered the one accessory I *had* packed—the marvelous silver dancing shoes I'd bought. I hadn't worn them yet. They'd be perfect, too.

I thought about the conversation I'd had with Julie about the shoes. I'd told her they would help the guy of my dreams find me on the dance floor. *I wasn't wrong, either*, I told myself smugly as I got into bed. *Tomorrow night a certain guy is going to see a brand-new girl* he *never dreamed of!*

Chapter Seven

I really felt like a new person the next evening as I stood in front of the mirror in my room. Actually, I felt like an old person—like the old Barrie Sampson who always had to be well-dressed and well-groomed before she stepped out of the house. The last couple of weeks at jockey school had almost destroyed my former ideas about makeup and clothes. I'd been satisfied with just having my hair tied out of the way, and being halfway clean!

Now, though, I was thrilled with the way I looked. Christy's long silvery scarf knotted around my waist exactly matched my new silver shoes. I'd spent ages putting on my makeup and styling my freshly washed hair. I'd let my hair hang loose and held it back from my face with two combs. I had to admit, I looked pretty fantastic.

Paul must have thought so, too, because he let out a whistle when he saw me. He looked great, too, in neat khaki pants, a pale blue shirt, and a navy blue blazer. Just as he'd always seen me in jeans, I'd always seen him in his work clothes. The sight of him all dressed up was a real surprise. I couldn't help but wonder what other surprises he had in store for me.

Paul had his own car, a beat-up Chevy sedan. As I might have expected, he was an excellent driver. The trip into town took only about fifteen minutes, and Paul immediately found a parking place right in front of The Topping.

It looked just like old pictures I'd seen of ice-cream parlors around the turn of the century. There was lots of stained glass, a marble-topped counter, lighting fixtures that looked like gas lamps, and waitresses in old-fashioned dresses. On the small dance floor, some couples were dancing to rock music, the only modern touch in the place.

Paul guided me to a quiet booth in the back. "At least we won't have the music blasting at us here," he said as he slid in beside me.

"Good idea," I agreed. The menu looked fantastic. I tried to figure out how many different flavors of ice cream I could eat without gaining too much weight.

Paul obviously sensed what I was thinking. "Might as well go for it," he advised. "You'll work it all off tomorrow anyway."

When our waitress came over, I ordered a hot-fudge sundae with chocolate, butter pecan, and maple walnut ice cream, plus whipped cream, nuts, and a cherry. Paul laughed when my enormous sundae arrived. "I can't believe you'll finish that all by yourself," he said. He'd asked for a chocolate ice-cream soda, and he began sipping while I dug into my sundae.

"Alone at last," I said, smiling at him. "Now I want you to tell me everything about yourself. You've been at Rolling Meadows for about a year, right?"

"Actually more like fifteen months," Paul replied. "I'm hoping to go straight from here to a job with a trainer at a racetrack."

"When?"

"Oh, a few more months. I have to wait for an opening."

"You certainly seem ready to me," I told him. I'd seen Paul riding the horses on the track at school. His position was always perfect, and he seemed in tune with whichever mount he rode. He was the best rider I'd ever seen.

"You're getting pretty good yourself," Paul said. "Did you ride a lot before you came here?"

I shook my head. "Whenever I come to visit Christy and Harv, they let me ride their horses. And there's a stable at home where I ride sometimes. But this is the first time I've ever ridden on a regular basis."

"Well, you ought to be proud of yourself then," Paul told me. "Dutch is really impressed with how much you've learned. He said you're making progress faster than anyone in the class."

"Really?" I was delighted to hear that—and pretty surprised as well. "But he always acts as though I'm way behind. Nothing I do seems to be good enough for him."

"Don't you believe it. He's keeping an eye on you and pushing you because he knows you're good. You've got a natural way with horses, Barrie. They like you and trust you. That's half the battle right there."

I blushed. I could hardly believe I was sitting with Paul Kaufman hearing him tell me how great I was. It was like a dream come true! I loved being with him. Now that we'd broken the ice, I discovered how easy he was to talk to. I'd gone out with a lot of other guys back home who spent the whole evening talking about themselves or treating me like a thing, not a person. Paul was completely different.

He finally told me something about his life away from the track. I found out that Paul lived only about ten miles from Rolling Meadows and sometimes spent his Sundays off with his parents. It had been his father's idea for Paul to become a jockey. "Good idea, too," Paul told me. "After all, if you want your kid to be an athlete, but he's only about five six, you can't expect him to take up football or basketball."

Someone must have turned up the music, because suddenly I could hear one of my favorite rock songs blaring out of the speakers. The dance floor at the front of the club began to fill up.

"Want to dance?" Paul asked me. Leaving the rest of my sundae, I nodded and slid out of the booth. Hand in hand, we moved toward the center of the floor.

Paul was as graceful on the dance floor as he was on a horse, and the music had a great beat. I really love to dance, and it was great having a partner as good as Paul. He didn't step on my feet or bump into me once. After a while I just closed my eyes and let the rhythm carry me away. I was having the best time of my entire life. Then I heard a giggle. I opened my eyes. The giggle came from a girl a few feet away. She was wearing a slinky yellow dress and high, high heels. She was dancing with a guy who looked like a football player and who towered over her.

But the strangest thing about her was that the girl seemed to be laughing at me. I couldn't figure it out. Had my dress come unhooked? Was my face smeared with fudge sauce?

Then I saw her eyes travel to Paul. The giggle got even louder. I glanced behind him at our reflection in the mirrored walls, and then I knew exactly why she was so amused.

The heels of my beautiful silver dancing shoes added an extra two or three inches to my height, which meant that tonight Paul was actually shorter than I. No wonder the girl in yellow thought we looked funny together. She and all the other girls were dancing with much taller boys. By contrast, I looked like a giraffe.

Furtively, I looked around the dance floor. Nobody else was laughing, but I saw other girls glance in our direction. One or two gave me bright, pitying smiles. Others just smirked and looked away.

I remembered my first day at jockey school, when I'd first realized Paul was a lot shorter than the six-foot hunk I'd pictured in my fantasies. I'd always dreamed of dating a big, husky guy who would wrap his brawny arms around me and make me feel utterly protected. I watched the other girls on the dance floor with their big, husky dates. *That* was exactly the kind of guy I'd wanted. . . .

The music changed to a slow number. The other girls snuggled into their boyfriends' arms. Paul smiled and reached out for me, but suddenly I couldn't dance anymore. If we looked funny together just dancing apart, I couldn't imagine what we'd look like with our arms around each other. I tried to picture us dancing like that, and in my mind we looked just plain silly, nothing like the other couples around us. And I hated the idea that the other girls were feeling sorry for me because I was out with a short guy.

Paul started to take my hand, but I pulled away. "No, let's sit down. I'm—I'm tired." Without waiting for him, I headed across the floor toward our booth.

The girl in yellow smiled nastily as I passed and murmured, "What's the matter? Couldn't find a date your own size?"

I couldn't believe it. Nobody had ever made an insulting remark to me before, especially not someone I'd never even met. I was furious.

I was just about to take a good yank at that slinky yellow dress when Paul came up quickly behind me. "Hi, how are you?" he said to the girl and her date. One of his arms went around my waist, and he tried to drag me away. I didn't move. I was still glaring at the girl, still wanting to snatch at that yellow dress till it tore apart right in front of everybody. She had no right to talk to me like that. Most of all, she had no right to say mean things about Paul!

"What's up, Barrie?" he asked quietly.

I tried to shrug off my anger. "Nothing." I turned away. I didn't want Paul to know what was going on. He was too wonderful to be hurt by such an awful person.

The girl in yellow looked down at Paul and sneered, "Isn't he *cute*?"

I could tell Paul knew just what she meant, because his ears reddened. For a second he glared at her. Then he got himself under control. He even managed a trace of his usual sunny smile. "Glad you think so. You're pretty cute, yourself. Sorry I can't ask you to dance. Maybe next year, when you grow up a little more, huh?" Then he chucked her under the chin.

I couldn't help laughing. It was really the perfect put-down. As I saw her face turn red, my anger dissolved, and my admiration for Paul increased.

We left a few minutes later. I was very quiet as Paul drove, realizing how stupidly I'd reacted. I'd actually let some dumb girl I'd never seen make me feel bad about being with Paul, whom I really cared about. He didn't look like a football player, but so what? I didn't need a huge, muscular guy. Paul made me feel special and protected even if he wasn't six feet tall. He was gorgeous and kind and bright and hardworking, and I was a very lucky girl, because of all the girls at Rolling Meadows he could have dated, he'd taken me out.

I was so preoccupied with these thoughts that I didn't realize that Paul wasn't saying a word. He stopped the car at Christy and Harv's front door. I turned to say good night with a smile but stopped cold. Paul was sitting at the steering wheel, staring straight ahead as if I weren't there.

"Well, uh—thanks a lot . . ." I began. When he didn't respond, I started to feel very uncomfortable. "I had a great time. The Topping's a terrific place."

"See you tomorrow," Paul answered, still looking straight ahead as he spoke.

"Paul, is something wrong?" I whispered.

"No." He wouldn't meet my eyes. He was acting like a total stranger.

Really upset now, I said, "Paul, what is it?"

He still wouldn't turn to face me. I reached over to touch his arm, but with one flick of his wrist, he shook my hand off. I suddenly felt ice-cold inside. "You better go in," he said. "It's late. You're due at feed at five-thirty."

"I'll be there," I answered automatically. My heart was doing funny flip-flops in my chest, and I felt sick. Paul was acting as if he couldn't wait to get away from me, and I didn't have any idea why, or what to do.

Finally, helpless, I got out of the car. An instant later it roared away. Paul didn't even wait to see if I'd gotten inside.

I slowly climbed the stairs to my room, trying to figure out what had gone wrong. The problem was, I didn't have a clue. So how could I know how to fix it?

Chapter Eight

"What is backtracking?" Dutch asked the next day during our classroom session.

"Backtracking," Tessa recited, "is running a horse in the direction opposite of the usual racetrack pattern. Since American racetracks usually run counterclockwise, backtracking here means running the horse on a clockwise course."

"Very good, Tessa." Dutch looked at me. I was hunched over my notebook, hoping he wouldn't call on me. "All right, Barrie. Your turn. Run through the steps of grooming a racehorse."

I blinked. "The steps of . . . okay. First you tie the horse to a stall tie, to keep him from moving around too much. Then—" I stopped suddenly, because Paul had appeared in the doorway to the classroom.

"Dutch, there's a girl asking for you in the

office," he said. "She says you're expecting her today."

"Right." Dutch stood up. "Paul, stay and conduct the rest of their lesson, will you? I'll go on up to the office now."

Paul nodded to Dutch and sat down at the table, where we were all sitting with our notebooks open. I peeked at him out of the corner of my eye, but Paul deliberately turned away from me and talked only to Tessa. "Where were you?"

"Barrie was describing the steps in grooming a racehorse," Tessa said.

"Good. Go on." Paul looked down at his clasped hands when he spoke to me, which only made me feel worse, if that was possible. It was bad enough that I'd spent all of last night feeling sick and miserable. Now it looked as if Paul and I probably wouldn't speak to each other again all summer, except about the stable work. That thought made me feel even sicker and more miserable.

I forced myself to go over the steps again, but Paul interrupted me. "Say *why* you do each thing. It's important to know why you're doing what you're doing."

"Okay." I wanted to look him full in the face and smile, but his coldness made it impossible. Part of me wanted to beg him to tell me what was wrong. The other part was determined not to speak unless he spoke first.

As I detailed the steps, I found myself forgetting things I did automatically every day, not to mention why. I was so nervous, I couldn't keep my mind on what I was saying.

"What do you do after using the hoof pick?" Paul pressed.

His tone made me even more flustered. "Well, uh—you—you medicate the horse's hooves—"

"Wrong," Paul interrupted. "You should know these steps by now, Barrie. Can't you keep your mind on what you're doing?" He turned to Jo. "All right, Jo. What's the next step after the hoof pick?"

"The soft brush," Jo said promptly. "You use it on the hooves to clean out any remaining dirt."

"Good." Paul stood up, shut the notebook in front of him, and stuck it under his arm. "Okay, classroom work's over for the day. Barrie, you'd better write out the steps of grooming a horse. Bring them to class tomorrow. Dutch'll want to be sure you know the entire procedure."

"I *do* know it," I said hotly, as the other kids were leaving. "You *know* I know it. You taught it to me!"

Finally Paul looked at me. His usually warm dark eyes were flat and cold. "I guess I didn't do a great job then, did I? Write it out for tomorrow." Without another word he turned his back on me and walked out of the room.

Most of the morning stable work had been done already. The laundry had been washed, and I volunteered to hang it on the line to dry. It wasn't a fun job, but at least it meant I could be alone for a few minutes. I didn't want to have to explain to anyone why my eyes kept brimming over with tears. There was a lot to hang, and I didn't return to the stable area for some time. When I did, I found the rest of the student jockeys gathered around someone new.

She was petite, probably not more than five two, with a mane of soft blond hair and a delicate, feminine figure. She looked to be about seventeen. She had the kind of face I'd always envied, naturally pretty even without makeup, and a model-perfect smile. Even the freckles scattered on her pert nose were cute.

"Barrie," Dutch called to me, "come on over and meet Heather, my niece. She'll be spending some time here at Rolling Meadows."

"Hi," I said, hoping my voice didn't still sound husky from crying. "Nice to meet you."

"Oh, nice to meet you, too," Heather replied. "I'm so glad to meet all Uncle Dutch's students."

"Do you want to become a jockey, too?" I asked.

Heather gave me a superior smile. "Oh, I'm

not going to *study* here, if that's what you mean. I've already got my exercise rider's license."

"Congratulations," I said politely. "That's great."

"Yes," Heather went on. "Uncle Dutch thought it would be a good idea for his students to see an example of a really *good* rider. He thinks it'll inspire the rest of you."

I heard what sounded like a snort behind me and turned. Marla was polishing one of the saddles with leather cleaner, but she managed to give me a look that said exactly what she thought of the new arrival. I rolled my eyes in agreement.

Dutch introduced Heather the next morning as his assistant riding instructor, who would teach classes when he was busy. "Heather just got her exercise rider's license and is working at the Maryleigh track," he told us all at the morning meeting. "She has the dedication and talent you should all be striving for. I want you to watch her ride and learn from her."

"Yes, by all means," Heather said sweetly to all of us. "And remember, it's not important that you don't ride as well as I do. We all have different levels of ability, and each of you can reach yours, whatever it is," she finished. "After all, I had to work hard for many years to achieve the riding level I'm at now."

"Well, I'm glad she was working on her riding at least," Jo whispered to me. "We know she wasn't working on her personality."

I giggled. Heather fixed me with a frozen stare. "Now I want to see you all ride this morning," she went on. "Then I'll know just how much time to give each of you." She glared at me. "I'm sure *some* of you need more attention than others."

"Can you believe that girl?" Greg exclaimed that afternoon after lunch. He, Tessa, Jo, Marla, and I were sitting with cold sodas on the steps of the girls' dormitory. "She wanted me to post without irons for ten minutes straight, and when I finally told her I was getting tired, she said in that sweetsy-poo voice of hers, 'Well, all I know is, no professional *ever* admits he's tired. I hope you're not going to take that attitude with you to the track.' "

"She's the pits," Jo agreed. "She told me I should always belly up in the saddle and never wait for a leg up from someone else." Jo imitated Heather's voice. " 'Who knows, Jo, someday there just might not be someone else there to cover for you.' *Cover* for me! That's what Dutch taught us, didn't he?"

"Want a treat?" Bobby said, coming over from the stables. "Heather's riding in the training ring. She told me you should all come out to watch, so you can pick up some pointers."

"I can think of a pointer I'd like to give *her*," I snapped.

Marla stood up wearily. "Might as well go and watch. Who knows, maybe we'll get lucky and she'll fall off!"

We all trudged out to the ring and settled in the bleachers. There was Heather, working with Satin Girl, one of the school horses. She had set up plastic cones in an obstacle course, and now she guided Satin Girl around the cones at a trot.

Satin Girl was the horse I usually rode, and I knew how tough she could be. She hated to gallop or even hobby, which was the racing term for cantering. Most of the time I had to work at keeping up her speed.

Heather looked up and saw us watching. "Okay," she called. "Now we'll try the same course at a little faster pace."

"Good luck," I mumbled. I hoped Satin Girl would refuse to change her gait, making Heather look like a fool in front of all of us. Anybody who was that conceited deserved to be humiliated!

I could hardly believe my eyes when Heather smoothly shifted Satin Girl into a hobby and then to a full-out gallop. She took the mare through the course again and again. Satin Girl never once broke her stride, and she cut so close to the cones that even Bobby let out a whistle of appreciation.

Marla and I looked at each other in disgust. It was bad enough that the little show-off was going to be teaching us with Dutch's blessing. It was even worse that she really could ride better than any of us. And that still wasn't the most awful thing about her.

Marla nudged me. "Look at Paul," she whispered. "I think he's hypnotized."

I looked down. Paul was leaning on the fence that went around the ring, and his eyes were locked on Heather in total concentration. By now Heather had kicked her feet out of the stirrups and was demonstrating how to post without the support of the irons. It was much harder to keep your balance that way, but Heather looked as carefree as though she were sitting on a rocking horse.

"Show-off!" I whispered angrily, but it wasn't really Heather that I was mad at. Except when he criticized my classroom work, Paul hadn't spoken to me at all for two days. Now here he was, looking at Heather as though he wanted to eat her up. It was obvious that he was very impressed with her riding, and maybe with her pretty blond hair and cute freckles as well. Suddenly I felt really sick inside.

I got up and blindly stumbled off the bleachers. "You all right, Barrie?" Tessa asked as I passed her.

"No. I'm going up to the dorm for a minute. I think I better lie down. Must be the sun . . ." Without even looking around, I hurried toward the dorms. I was going to either burst into tears or throw up, and either way I didn't want anybody else to see it. I had a feeling that my problems with Paul were about to get worse. *Much* worse!

Chapter Nine

"All right, Barrie—*again!*" Heather called. I was hobbying Satin Girl around the training ring. "Post without irons for as long as you can."

I gritted my teeth. I hated posting without stirrups. It always made my legs ache, even though I was much stronger now than when I'd first arrived. Heather obviously knew it, too. I wasn't going to complain, though. If she wanted to make me quit, she'd have to push me a lot harder than that.

As I kicked my feet out of the stirrups, I heard Heather say, "Oh, Paul, I'm so glad you're here! I thought of something I wanted to tell you after our talk last night."

Their talk last night? I felt a pang of jealousy tear right through me. What had they talked about? And for how long? Did it end up with their kissing good night? I didn't want to think about it, but my mind wouldn't let go of the idea. I could almost see them with their arms wrapped around each other. It was a horrible picture.

As Satin Girl turned and trotted toward the end of the ring, I could see Heather and Paul standing close together and talking quietly. For an instant, as I watched them, Paul looked at me. Then he turned his eyes away quickly and went on speaking to Heather. I tried to tell myself I wasn't upset, but the next second I lost my posting balance and plopped down heavily in the saddle.

"I just don't know *what* to do with her," I heard Heather declare to Paul. "She doesn't seem to get it at all."

I wondered how it would feel to pull out every strand of Heather's perfect silky blond hair. Then I decided I'd better not think about it. The idea was much too tempting.

The whole week had been absolutely miserable. I'd seen Heather every single day for my riding instruction. It used to be my favorite part of the day, but now I was beginning to hate it. Nothing I did ever pleased Heather, and she never lost the chance to make some cutting remark about my clumsiness or lack of attention. "If you'd just *think* about what you're doing," she'd sigh, "I know you could do so much better." It sounded as if she thought I could hardly do much worse!

It was even harder seeing her around Paul. After watching all of us ride, Heather had announced that Paul was without a doubt the most talented rider among us. That wasn't surprising. What was surprising was that Heather had asked Dutch for special permission to tutor Paul herself. Privately.

The other kids saw right through her. "What a great way for her to be alone with him every day." Greg smirked. "Paul better watch out!"

"Oh, I don't know," Bobby said. "I don't think I'd mind if a girl that good-looking wanted to be alone with me an hour or two every day. In fact, I might just start to look forward to it."

Bobby was right. Heather not only rode superbly, she also looked like a model every hour of the day. It was awful for me to sweat through my morning chores in my T-shirt and jeans, and then see Heather in her neat jodhpurs and shining black boots, looking so cool and pretty. It was no wonder Paul spent so much of his time with her.

I tried to ignore it, but it was hard not to notice. Heather and Paul were always either talking together, laughing, or sitting together on breaks. I wondered if he'd let her in on his Alfie secret. Maybe—the thought nearly killed me—they pretended to cross the finish line together.

Paul hadn't even tried to talk to me since the night of our disastrous date. He did his work and chatted and joked with the other jockeys the way he always had. But he had nothing to say to me.

One day Paul and I were inspecting and cleaning tack together. Everyone else was busy working with the horses or raking up the stable yard. Paul worked on one stack of equipment while I worked on the other. He was whistling under his breath. I swallowed my pride and decided to try to talk to him.

"How's your riding?" I asked politely. "Are you learning a lot from Heather?"

Paul glanced at me for a second, then looked down at the bridle in his hands. "She knows a lot," he mumbled.

"I'm sure she does," I agreed. I didn't want to argue with him, especially about Heather. "Do you think it's helping your riding?"

He shrugged. "Everything you learn helps your riding."

"I guess." I hesitated, then took the plunge. "Look, are you mad at me for something? We haven't really talked since the night we went to The Topping, and I don't know what's wrong."

"Nothing's wrong." Paul took the clean bridle into the tack room and returned to work on another one.

"Sure there is," I insisted. "I thought we— well, we used to *talk* about things. You used to help me with my riding."

Paul turned to me, a flash of anger in his eyes. "Is that what this is all about? You miss having a tutor at your beck and call all the time?"

"That's not what I meant," I started to protest, but he cut me off.

"Look, it's part of my job to help the new students. So I took you out. Don't make a big deal out of it, okay?"

I felt as if I'd been slapped. Was that all our date was to him—a way to help the new girl? I'd thought we were starting to be friends, maybe even more than that. Had I been mistaken?

"I'm not asking for help," I began again.

"Good. I haven't got much time these days. In fact, I need more hours with Heather than I'm getting." Paul tossed the bridle over his shoulder. "Finish up the rest, will you? I've got to check the feed." He walked away without looking back.

"He hates me!" I wailed to Christy that night. She and Harv were trying to watch television, but I was so miserable that I couldn't help interrupting. Finally Harv clicked off the TV set, and Christy looked at me thoughtfully.

"He sure doesn't sound like the guy I met at the barbecue," she said.

"Nothing's been the same since the night we went out," I went on. "And it's been worse since Heather got there. She's out to get him, I know she is!"

Harv stretched out in his lounge chair.

"Well, she won't get him unless he wants her to."

"You don't know her," I said unhappily. "Not only is she really gorgeous, she's also a terrific rider."

"With a prize-winning personality." Christy grinned. "Paul seems like a pretty smart guy. He should be able to see through that sugary exterior to what's underneath."

"All he thinks about is his riding." I sighed.

"Then maybe that's what you should be thinking about." Christy sat up abruptly. "Come on. I've got a terrific craving for popcorn. Let's make some."

I never could figure out how Christy could eat the way she did and still keep her trim figure. In a few minutes all three of us were pouring melted butter over fresh popcorn and digging in with both hands.

I smiled for what seemed like the first time in weeks. "Christy, how'd you know this stuff would make me feel better?"

She shrugged. "It always makes *me* feel better." I was hardly listening. Then, suddenly something she'd said to me earlier clicked. I realized she'd given me the answer to my problem.

"Hey, say what you said before. About the riding."

"What? That you should be thinking about it, too?"

"It makes sense, doesn't it?" I munched on

the buttery popcorn and thought about it. "Since that's what Paul thinks about most, how else could I get his attention except by becoming a better rider?"

Harv smiled. "It's been known to work. Besides, you'll be a better rider at the end of the summer only if you put in more hours."

"Harv, you're a genius!" I gave him a big, buttery hug.

"Aw, you just say that 'cause it's true," he said modestly.

I'd give Heather a run for her money. It was true that I didn't have lovely blond hair or a perfect face or a riding style that would knock Paul's socks off. If there was one thing I did have, though, it was determination. Once I threw myself into something, I always got what I wanted. I decided to start the next day. I'd make faster and more noticeable progress than any student Dutch had ever had. Paul wouldn't be able to ignore me once he saw how good I was!

"Barrie, for heaven's sake, it's almost nine!" Marla protested as I worked on Alfie a few nights later.

I frowned. "So? I still can't post without irons for ten minutes straight."

"You've been working on it for hours," Marla complained. "Isn't that enough for one night?"

"Just a little while longer. Come on, Marla."

"It's movie night up at Dutch's house," she reminded me. "You don't want to miss it, do you?"

"Believe me, I want to go. But I just *have* to get this down."

Marla slid down against the stall door and sat in the straw. "You're going to work yourself to death," she said. "Then what?"

I laughed. "Maybe I'll get the 'Student of the Month' award."

"Terrific," she retorted. "We'll hang your picture in the tack room. Personally, I don't think it's worth the effort, even if you are trying to win Paul back from Miss Bimbo."

I stared at her in surprise. I'd really hoped no one noticed how I felt about Paul. Had I been that obvious?

"Hey, it's okay," Marla tried to comfort me. "We all thought you guys were kind of cute together. In fact, we thought—"

"Yeah, I know," I said glumly. "I kind of thought so myself."

"I've changed my mind. If that's why you're doing it, go for it. I can't stand Heather. She's not nearly good enough for Paul."

"And I am?"

"Actually," Marla said with a smile, "the question is whether *he's* good enough for *you*. But if he's what you want, okay!" She glanced at her watch, and once more I started lifting myself out of the saddle without using the irons. I'd end the summer as either a great exercise rider or a hopeless cripple.

What happened a few days later made all the practice worthwhile.

Dutch held his usual morning meeting with us before we began the day's work. The horses had been fed, but he never gave out assignments until he talked to us about the business of horse racing. We all crowded into the classroom to listen.

"Great news," Dutch announced. "You all know about the Wellspring Fair?" A few of us looked blank, so he explained. "It's held every year at the beginning of August. There are lots of different events: animal exhibits, booths with homemade jellies and baked goods, and a few special shows. This year they're also having a pony race, which will be about a mile long. The ponies belong to the local people, and they want good young amateur jockeys to ride them."

You could hear a pin drop in the room. Everybody wanted the chance to ride in that race! Dutch looked around for a minute, then went on. "There are spots open for two riders from Rolling Meadows. Obviously we'll want to send our best."

Heather tossed her mane of golden hair and smiled engagingly at her uncle. "It's too bad the race is for amateurs. Otherwise, I'd easily qualify."

No one dared to say what they thought in front of Dutch. But even he looked a little embarrassed. He cleared his throat awkwardly. "Well, since it is amateurs only, I've decided on two riders here who should have a chance to participate—if they want to. They don't have to, but I think it would be good practice. Paul is my first choice."

There were nods and smiles all around. Greg and Bobby slapped Paul on the back. He grinned his acceptance at Dutch, who continued. "The second rider hasn't been here very long, but she's made excellent progress." He paused. "The second rider is going to be—Barrie."

I gasped. I couldn't believe Dutch thought I was good enough to ride in a real race! Wendy and Jo leaned over to hug me and whisper congratulations, and Marla squeezed my hand and smiled at me.

Dutch looked directly at me. "If you want to do it, Barrie, the spot's yours. Either way, as of today you move up to the advanced class. From now on you ride on the track, not in the training ring."

I was almost in shock as he went on. "Barrie's a good example of what I keep telling all of you. She's out there every night, working on Alfie after putting in a full day at school. That's how you get ahead, boys and girls. It ain't good looks, and it ain't good luck that'll get you there. It's hard work and perseverance. Barrie's got both. She'll make a good exercise rider, maybe even as soon as the end of the summer."

Then Dutch gave out the morning assignments and everyone filed out. I couldn't resist hanging back for a moment to thank him. "I'm so excited, Dutch! This is almost the best thing that's happened to me this summer."

He smiled at me. "Well, you earned it, kid. Tell you the truth, I thought for the first few days you were gonna quit. You seemed more like a party girl than a hard worker." He put a hand on my shoulder. "Glad I was wrong."

"You weren't," I told him. "That's just what I was before this summer. My parents won't believe this when I tell them. They probably won't even *recognize* me when I go home!"

"Uh—Barrie." Dutch stopped me as I turned to leave. "We have one little problem here."

"Problem?"

"Not about the race," Dutch assured me. "You'll ride in that, all right. It's about Heather."

I can sure understand that, I thought. But I didn't know what was coming.

"Listen, we're filled up here, and there may be some new students coming in the next few days. At your barbecue your aunt suggested I send any overflow of students to stay with her. You think she'd mind if I sent Heather over?"

I stared at him in dismay. I didn't want to sleep in the same house with that conceited little airhead. *Please don't do this to me!* I cried inwardly.

I was speechless. What I *wanted* to say was that I hated Heather and didn't want to see her at school, let alone at the farm, because she was arrogant and superior and smug— not to mention after the guy who had broken my heart. Of course, I couldn't tell Dutch any of that, so I kept my mouth shut.

Evidently Dutch thought my silence meant it was okay. With a sigh of relief, he said, "Well, fine. I'll call Christy this morning. Maybe she'll let Heather move in tonight. Thanks, Barrie." He walked out to the stables.

I leaned against the door frame, horrified. It didn't seem possible that this nightmare was happening! I could already picture Heather sitting at the dinner table with Christy and Harv and me, bragging about her incomparable riding skills and her relationship with Paul. What if they went out on dates? What if I had to see them kissing good night under my very own window? How was I going to stand any of it?

Chapter Ten

"What a darling room!" Heather gushed that evening. She'd been disgustingly nice to both Christy and Harv when she arrived, thanking them in her most sugary voice for taking her in. Then Christy had shown her to one of the smaller rooms on the third floor. I was glad I didn't have to share my room with her. I think I would have ended up pushing her out a window if I had.

"I hope everything's all right," Christy told her. "The linen closet's right outside your door if you need more blankets or anything. We usually have dinner around six-thirty, when Barrie gets home."

"Oh, that's fine. I won't be eating much anyway. I've got to lose about six pounds as soon as I can."

Christy stared at Heather's tiny frame. "Which six did you want to get rid of?" I couldn't help giggling. Christy had such a funny way of putting things.

Heather surveyed herself in the mirror over the bureau. "It's for professional reasons, of course. I can't afford to weigh more than about ninety-eight pounds at the most."

"I thought exercise riders were allowed to weigh more than jockeys," Christy said. "At least, that's what Barrie told us."

"Oh, and she's absolutely right, Mrs. Allison." I could have gagged at the way Heather was sucking up to my aunt. "But I intend to be a jockey in a couple of years, so it won't look good if I carry too much weight now. Besides," she sighed theatrically, "I might as well get used to depriving myself. After all, that's what I'll be doing for the rest of my life."

Christy shot me a mischievous look. "Well, Heather, we certainly understand. I'm sorry I didn't know that you were dieting. We're having homemade ice cream for dessert tonight, with whipped cream, nuts, and sprinkles. Too bad you'll have to miss it." The fleeting look of regret on Heather's face made me feel a lot better, until she spoke up again.

"Oh, but I'm sure Barrie won't want any either, Mrs. Allison. After all, she *is* riding in her first race next week. It would be a shame if she lost because she was too heavy for her pony." The little witch was right, too. She had me backed into a corner, and we both knew it. I loathed her more than ever.

"I wish you'd never made that offer to Dutch!" I hissed at Christy later, in the privacy of my room. "What if Paul starts dating her? How am I going to stand seeing him come here to pick her up?"

Christy was very sorry, but as usual, she was also practical. "We don't know that he will date her, Barrie. All we really know is that she's out to get him. That's a big difference. They may not see each other at all outside of school."

I hoped not. Just sitting at the dinner table with Heather strained my patience. While I loaded up on salad, determined not to eat more than she did even if I starved to death, Heather babbled away.

"Oh, yes, Mr. Allison, Uncle Dutch helped train me for the track. He's always said I was the only natural rider he's ever known, and I'm a wonderful example to his students." She nibbled daintily on a lettuce leaf. "I'm not riding in the pony race. It's an amateur race, you see, and since I'm so much better than the other riders, it would give me too much of an advantage as a jockey."

After that announcement Christy and Harv said little beyond "Pass the rolls." I said nothing and kept my eyes on my plate, though what I really wanted to do was choke Heather with my bare hands. I began to realize that

I would never have a weight problem as long as she was around. Listening to her made me completely lose my appetite.

At school I concentrated harder than ever on my training. Riding on the track was a whole new experience, and I took to it right away. I began to sense when another horse was coming up behind or beside mine and to feel the temperament of the horse I rode. I could almost forget my problems as I rode in the fresh air in the early mornings and smelled the flowers planted along the rail. Riding on the track, I felt like a real jockey at last.

I also saw Paul every single day. We often raced each other for practice, with Dutch shouting instructions from the bleachers by the rail. Dutch spent long hours with Paul and me, instructing us on race strategy. Luckily he didn't trust Heather to give us pointers on this subject, so I didn't have to watch her flirting with Paul during my riding hours.

Ever since that afternoon when Paul had lashed out at me, I'd been unable to think of any way to talk to him. Once in a while, as we lined up our horses for a practice race, he'd yell something friendly to me, just the way he used to: "Come on, Barrie, try not to *stroll* down to the wire!" or "Think you'll beat me when you're closer to the ground?" But by the time we got to the finish line, he was morose and silent again.

Heather spent most of her free hours hanging around the stable, telling Paul about her experiences as an exercise rider. "We have so much to discuss," she'd say to the others if they wanted to talk to Paul. "Do you *have* to speak to him right now?" I noticed that Paul spent a lot of his time with her talking about trainers and tracks. And instead of going off to be alone with her, he joined in the jockeys' parties and get-togethers a lot more often than he had in the past. Maybe, I hoped, he wasn't as fascinated by Heather as she wanted us all to believe.

"I think we should celebrate Barrie's first race, don't you, honey?" Christy asked Harv a few nights later. Heather had gone to take a shower, so for once just the three of us were in the den.

"Definitely," Harv agreed. "It's a pretty big deal. What kind of celebration did you have in mind?"

Christy thought a moment, then said, "How about a barn dance next Friday night?"

I loved the idea of a real barn dance the night before the race. Even Heather bubbled over with excitement when she heard about it and talked nonstop about what she could wear to such a special event. For the first time I was glad she was so much smaller

107

than I. That meant she couldn't borrow any of my clothes.

The week before the race, Dutch spent extra time with Paul and me. He timed our gallops and showed us some race footage he kept on videotapes. "See how the jockey took advantage of that hole?" he kept saying. "You've got to watch for your opportunities. If you don't see them, you have to create them yourself."

By the night of the barn dance, Harv and Christy's barn looked like a brand-new place, thanks to all the work the three of us had done fixing it up. (Naturally, Heather hadn't helped at all.) There were old-fashioned lanterns hanging from pegs in the walls, and bales of hay were piled here and there for people to sit on. Harv had swept the floor until it was clean and perfect for dancing. Christy and I covered a long wooden table with a red-and-white checked tablecloth and set out bowls of ice-cold fruit punch, platters of cupcakes and cookies, and raw vegetables and dip for those of us who needed to watch our figures. Harv's turntable and speakers stood on a table in one corner, along with a stack of records that included everything from square-dance music to hard and soft rock.

The dance was supposed to be "country casual," but I wanted to look my very best.

More than anything, I wanted to make Paul Kaufman sit up and take notice. After a great deal of thought, I decided to wear a full cotton skirt and a halter in a blue bandanna print. Christy loaned me a pair of wild silver earrings that dangled almost to my shoulders, and I wound my hair into a bun on top of my head. And even though I knew they were much too dressy for the occasion, I put on my silver dancing shoes.

"Wow!" Harv whistled in admiration when I came downstairs that evening. "Who's the gorgeous lady?"

"Think I'll give Heather a run for her money tonight?" I asked, twirling around for his inspection.

"As far as I'm concerned, there's never been any contest," Harv said, and gave me a hug.

Everyone started drifting in by about seven o'clock. I saw Dutch, in a Texas-style cowboy hat and checked shirt, arrive with Marla and Tessa, who were turned out in bright cotton shirts and full skirts much like mine. Wendy and Jo, who hadn't brought many dressy clothes to school, were wearing denim skirts and Rolling Meadows T-shirts. Bobby and Greg had on jeans and short-sleeved shirts.

I kept my eye out for Heather, who had stayed in her room until the very last minute. Naturally, when she finally appeared, she looked great. She'd tied her hair into a high ponytail with a wide scarlet satin ribbon that matched the tiny flowers in her off-the-shoulder calico dress. She wore a second ribbon as a belt, which emphasized her disgustingly narrow waist. It was even more depressing when I saw that she wasn't alone. Paul was right beside her, talking animatedly and looking more gorgeous than ever in faded jeans and a plaid shirt with the sleeves rolled up. I tried very hard to keep smiling, but seeing them together made it really hard.

Once everybody had arrived, Christy and Harv offered to teach us the basics of square dancing. While we crowded around, they showed us the steps and how to change partners, do-si-do, and promenade left and right.

Since there were so few of us, we all danced in one square. Unfortunately, Paul and Heather were partners, directly across from me and my partner, Greg. Wendy and Jo made up the third couple, and Marla and Bobby were the fourth, while Tessa and Dutch watched from the sidelines. When we danced around the square, swinging one person after another until we reached our places again, Paul would take my hand as though I were invisible. He never said a word to me or even smiled.

When the square-dancing music gave way to rock, some of the guests wandered over to the refreshment table. "Want to dance, Barrie?" Greg asked.

I noticed that Heather and Paul were still on the floor. And, as much as I hated to admit it, they made a great-looking couple. Heather was so small that Paul looked very tall standing next to her. I gritted my teeth. "Sure," I told Greg. "Why not?"

Greg had obviously done a lot of serious dancing, because in a moment we were doing some of the steps I'd seen in the movie *Dirty Dancing*. Greg was whirling me around so that my skirt billowed out from my legs and leading me through some pretty intricate dips and tips I'd never even seen before, let alone tried.

People on the sidelines cheered and applauded as we dipped and twirled. As I spun back from one turn, though, I bumped squarely into Paul, who was doing much more conventional steps with Heather. "Sorry!" I called to him.

The next instant I saw him reach for Heather's hand. "Let's get out of here. It's much too crowded," I heard him say in disgust. They left the floor at once, and I saw that their hands were still clasped as they strolled toward the refreshments.

Now Greg and I were alone on the floor. Although Greg looked as if he were ready to dance all night, I suddenly felt drained and completely miserable. I didn't want to be the center of attention anymore. I thought about how much I'd changed. The old me loved the spotlight, played up to her audience, and always looked for the most exciting place to be. But the new me was a girl who knew what she wanted, and what I wanted most right now was to be holding Paul's hand.

I cast a furtive eye at one corner of the barn, where Heather and Paul were now sitting cozily together on a hay bale. Heather was talking to him and gesturing excitedly as Paul watched her, smiling and sipping his punch. They were totally absorbed in each other. They didn't even look around the room.

I excused myself to Greg, wandered over to the turntable, and began to look through the records, reading their titles. When I finished with one stack of records, I started methodically with the second. I don't think I actually saw a single title, but it kept me from bursting into tears. The old song, "It's My Party and I'll Cry If I Want to" ran through my head. Now I knew exactly what the singer meant!

I looked down at the silver-strapped shoes I was wearing. I'd been so thrilled when I bought them, but each time I wore them, the event turned out to be a disaster. *Maybe I should give them to Julie when I get home,* I thought. *She might have better luck with them.*

"Barrie?" I turned my head and almost groaned. It was Heather. She grabbed my hand and tugged me away into a corner. "Listen, Paul and I are going back to Rolling Meadows for a little while. Would you mind telling your aunt where I am? I don't want her to worry."

Right, I thought. *But I bet you want me to worry a lot!* "It's getting late, Heather," I said. "You should come back pretty soon."

Heather giggled. When Paul came up behind her, she leaned back against him possessively. "Oh, I don't think we'll be very long. But if I'm not back in a few hours, leave the front door unlocked, okay? I don't want to wake anybody."

I couldn't believe that she was going off with Paul in the middle of my party. I wanted to scream, but somehow I managed to control myself. "If you're leaving, you'd better tell Dutch. He's responsible for you, after all."

"She doesn't need to tell anybody," Paul said shortly. "We're just going back to school. Besides, she's with me."

I was pretty fed up by now. "Oh, sure," I snapped. "I don't see that that's any guarantee of protection. If anything happens to Heather, Christy and Harv *and* Dutch will all have plenty to say about how responsible you are."

Then I stopped dead, suddenly regretting what I'd just said. I was saying anything that came into my head just to hurt Paul, and I didn't really want to do that. I cared about him too much.

The look on Paul's face was scary. His mouth drew into a long, straight line, and his dark eyes went even darker with anger. "Have I ever once acted irresponsibly?" he hissed at me. "Have I? In all the time you've known me? Have I ever said or done anything that I had to be ashamed of?" His hands clenched as though he were restraining himself from grabbing me and shaking me. He was completely different from the sunny, smiling, warm boy I'd gotten to know in my first weeks at school. He frightened me.

Heather looked from my face to Paul's. We were glaring at each other, neither of us willing to give an inch. Finally she put her hand on Paul's arm. "Come on, Paul. It'll be all right. I'm sure Barrie didn't mean to say that you couldn't be trusted. Come on. I want to see exactly how you throw those crosses."

Throw crosses? I thought furiously. *Does she really think I'll believe she's going off with Paul just to watch him demonstrate how he grips the reins on a racehorse? Fat chance!*

Paul's eyes never broke away from mine. They were cold and dark with rage. What he couldn't possibly know was how much I was already hurting inside.

As I watched them walk through the barn
door and disappear into the night, I didn't
think I'd ever felt worse in my life. And all
the music and laughter and good times in
the world weren't going to make me feel any
better.

Chapter Eleven

"There it is." Christy pointed at the sign near a cluster of buildings on the Wellspring fairgrounds the following day. "Jockeys Only. I guess that's you, Barrie."

"Thanks for the lift," I mumbled as I slid out of the Jeep. I was carrying a bag with my helmet and whip inside, and wearing a clean white shirt, my boots, and jodhpurs borrowed from Marla. I was determined to focus on the race ahead of me. *Forget everything else,* I told myself fiercely.

It wasn't easy. I'd kept smiling until my face ached at the party the night before, dancing and joking with everyone there for as long as I could stand it. When the party was almost over, I rushed up to my room, threw myself on the bed, and cried my eyes out. I was still awake when Heather came home a couple of hours later. I was glad she didn't come in to tell me all about her wonderful evening. If she had, I think I might have strangled her.

Forget all that, I repeated to myself. I was here to represent the school and do the very best I could. It didn't matter that Paul was one of the jockeys racing against me. As far as I was concerned, he was just one more jockey I had to beat.

The room set aside for the jockeys was large, divided into three sections. The girls' dressing room was on one side, and the boys' was on the other. In the open space in the center, several jockeys who were already dressed sat chatting. A couple of girls were bending and stretching to limber up, and some of the boys were doing breathing exercises.

I saw Paul right away. He was sitting on a bench by himself, wearing a bright green T-shirt and an arm band bearing the number two. He was looking at the ground. I thought he looked just as sad as I felt.

"Attention, jockeys!" I looked over to see a tall man wearing an official's badge who was clapping his hands for quiet. We all turned to him as he continued. "Welcome to the Wellspring Fair Pony Race. We're very excited about having you here, particularly the two newcomers from Rolling Meadows. We know it's going to be a great race!"

"And we also know who's going to win," smirked one of the older jockeys. He pointed to himself and took a bow. The rest of the riders groaned and yelled at him to sit down.

The man gestured for quiet. "You should have been issued colored T-shirts and arm bands with your post positions on them. If you haven't gotten them, make sure you check in at the officials' table to get them. When you've changed into your T-shirts, come out to the stable area. That's where you'll meet your mounts." He paused and looked around at us. "Good luck to you all."

Paul glanced up as I walked past him, but I didn't turn my head. What could I possibly say? It was better to concentrate on the race.

I signed in and received a neon pink T-shirt and an arm band with the number six on it. I quickly put on the T-shirt and tied on the arm band in the girls' dressing area and took my helmet and whip out of my bag. Then, following the others, I headed for the stable.

Dutch was already there, talking to the owner of my mount. He hailed me. "Here, Barrie. You'll be riding Greased Lightning."

"Greased Lightning?" I said a little doubtfully. The name didn't seem to fit the chubby little dapple gray pony standing in front of me.

Dutch grinned. "Think about all you've learned. You can make him fly!"

Lightning's owner, a man of about Dutch's age, came over to me. "He may not look like much, but he's got it through the legs. He'll give you a real good ride."

"Oh, Barrie's a pro," Dutch assured him.

The owner looked at me as doubtfully as I had at his pony. I wondered if he knew it was my first race. "Well, fine," he said. "See you at the finish line."

As he strode off, I murmured "Thanks" to Dutch. "It helps to hear that you think I'm a pro," I added.

"That's why I said it," he answered calmly. "I expect you to be right out there in front, Barrie. Start fast and keep this little guy moving. Don't look back till you hit the wire."

Just then came the call: "Jockeys up, please!" Dutch gave me a leg up, though it really wasn't necessary, and then I was ready to walk Greased Lightning down to the post. I saw Paul just ahead of me on a powerful-looking bay pony. He was adjusting the chin strap on his helmet. Although he sat tall and relaxed in the saddle, his face still looked unhappy.

Then the pony in front of his kicked out. Paul drew his mount back. Suddenly we were side by side. He looked at me, then away. Then he looked again. He started to open his mouth, as if he wanted to say something. I wanted to say a few things, too, but I didn't dare. I wanted to ask him if he and Heather had really gone back to school last night. I wanted to ask him if he liked Heather better than any other girl at Rolling Meadows, including me. Most of all, I wanted to ask him if we would ever be friends again.

"Good luck," I said at last. I figured he couldn't be offended by that.

Paul nodded. "You, too." I held my breath, waiting, but he didn't say any more. There didn't seem to be anything else to say. For a second I remembered the very first time we'd met, when he had rescued me at the track. I remembered how he'd smiled at me and asked whether I was all right, and I wanted to burst into tears right then and there.

Stop it, I told myself sternly. *You have a job to do. Think about the race.*

The ponies walked out of the stable so the spectators could look at them. I heard some familiar voices talking excitedly and turned my head to grin at the students from Rolling Meadows. Marla and Tessa waved at me and whistled, and Dutch gave me a thumbs-up sign.

Suddenly I felt a lot better. Dutch had believed in me—he'd given me this chance. The other jockeys had come out to cheer for me. They'd come to cheer for Paul, too, but the point was that they cared about how I did. Just the thought gave me a warm glow. I knew Christy and Harv had places near the finish line. I couldn't wait to see the look on their faces when I got there. I only hoped I'd get there first!

"Riders, please line up at the starting gate," came a voice over the loudspeaker. I trotted Lightning into the number six spot. Paul was in the number two lane to my left. I didn't even have to look over at him; I could feel his presence there. I looked straight down the broad track in front of me and narrowed my eyes in concentration.

A bell rang—and we were off! Greased Lightning leapt out in front of the pack at once. I had my whip out, but the pony didn't seem to need much prodding. He seemed to fly down the track! Gradually I heard the other ponies gaining on us. First a rider on my left came along, lashing his pony and yelling, "Go, go, go!" Then two riders on my right, crouched low on their mounts, tried to pull ahead.

I felt Greased Lightning beginning to slow down. "Oh, no, you don't!" I whispered. The finish line wasn't far off. I touched him with my whip, and the little gray pony moved faster. But the other ponies were closing in, and I realized that we'd started much too quickly. Lightning might not have enough drive left to win the race.

I coaxed him to an even faster pace and began to sense the others falling behind us again. Then I was aware of another rider moving up on my left.

It was Paul. He urged his pony forward, and the pony responded with all the power in his stocky little body. In a moment, I knew, Paul would leave me in the dust.

He did. Then other riders passed me on their mounts. There seemed to be a solid wall of horseflesh in front of us. Unless I did something fast, Greased Lightning and I were going to end up dead last in a race we'd been leading!

I spied a gap opening in the wall in front of us, a narrow space that we just might be able to squeeze through. I remembered Dutch's advice about creating opportunities in the race. If I could get through that gap, we still had a chance to take the lead again. I pushed Greased Lightning forward, closer and closer to the gap—

I never saw it coming. One of the riders had swerved his mount too close to another pony. When I tried to get into the gap, the three of us collided. I heard the groan of the crowd as I spun off Lightning and fell heavily in the dust.

Crack! Something hard and heavy came down on my leg. I looked up, shielding my face with my hands, and saw that it was Greased Lightning, who was floundering around, so confused and frightened that he'd stepped with his whole weight on my leg. I felt something snap. Then there was a flash of horrible pain, and I started to feel sick.

All around me I heard people shouting. Somebody came over and knelt beside me.

"You all right, young lady? How's that leg?" Someone else, I saw dimly through the dust, had grabbed Lightning's bridle and was talking to him quietly until the pony began to settle down.

There was a roar from the crowd at the finish line as the other ponies galloped across the wire. Then I heard a new sound, the sound of hooves pounding toward me and stopping abruptly. A rider flung himself out of the saddle and onto the track next to me.

"Barrie, are you okay?"

It was Paul.

For some reason the pain seemed worse when I opened my eyes, but I raised my lids just enough to see him kneel down next to me and take my hand. His skin looked chalky under the helmet. Paul held my hand tightly in both of his, and I could see him swallow hard before he said, "Barrie? Can you hear me? Do you know who I am?" I nodded feebly but had to close my eyes again. Everything was swimming in front of me.

Someone else knelt down and prodded gently at my leg. The pain was so intense that I screamed out loud. I opened my eyes in time to see Paul leap to his feet and grab the man who had touched me. "Stop it! Leave her alone! You're hurting her!"

"It's all right, son," said the tall race official we had met earlier. "That's Dr. Willis. He's just checking to see how much damage there is."

By now Christy and Harv were on the track, too, bending over me anxiously. "How bad is it?" Christy asked the doctor.

Dr. Willis shook his head. "I'm pretty sure there's a break. She should go to the hospital right away."

"I'll take her," Paul offered immediately. I shook my head dazedly. He was acting as though he cared what happened to me. As though he actually *cared* about me.

He took hold of my hand again and gave it a squeeze. "Listen, Barrie, it's going to be all right," he said gently. His dark brown eyes looked into mine for a long moment. In spite of the pain, I felt a warm, happy glow spread through me.

"What about the race?" I whispered. "Did you win?"

Paul hesitated, and the race official smiled. "He didn't even finish," he told me. "When he saw you were in trouble, he turned his horse around and came back to try to help you."

I couldn't believe it. Paul had given up his chance to win the race just to make sure I was all right. Knowing how competitive he was, I knew it could only mean one thing. He really *did* care about me!

There was some talk about getting an ambulance, the hospital, and X rays, but I didn't pay any attention. My leg was still throbbing, but the look on Paul's face as he watched me was the best painkiller in the world. Everything was going to be all right. There was no other place—not even first across the finish line—that I wanted to be.

Chapter Twelve

"Hold still just one more second," Dr. Willis said a while later. Then he stepped back from the table where I was lying in one of the hospital's treatment rooms. "Okay, we're all finished."

I peered down at the cast on my leg. It was big, white, and heavy. I'd never imagined that my great summer adventure would end like this!

An orderly pushed my wheelchair into the corridor where Christy, Harv, and Paul were anxiously waiting. "I'll take her back to the farm," Paul offered. "My car's pretty big. She can stretch out in the backseat. It'll be more comfortable than the Jeep."

My aunt and uncle didn't seem too sure about the idea, but I shot Christy a pleading look, and she got the message. "Okay. We'll go on ahead and get the den ready as a bedroom for you so you won't have to climb any stairs."

"Thanks," I whispered to her as she bent down and kissed my cheek. Harv pressed my hand comfortingly, and then they both left.

The orderly wheeled me down a ramp to the parking lot, and we waited while Paul drove his old sedan to the entrance and pulled up next to the curb. Paul got out and pushed the front seat forward. "I'll take care of everything," he told the orderly, then turned to me. "Just take it easy."

Before I knew what was happening, Paul lifted me out of the wheelchair and set me down carefully in the backseat. "I'll go real slow," he told me as he slid into the driver's seat. "If anything hurts, you be sure and let me know. Promise?"

"I promise."

"I was so scared when I saw you fall," Paul mumbled, turning the key in the ignition. "I didn't know what had happened to you. You could have broken your neck instead of your leg."

"Every jockey falls once in a while," I reminded him. It was something Dutch had told us over and over.

Paul smiled at me in the rearview mirror. "That's okay if I'm the one falling. But I can't stand the idea of you getting hurt."

"I thought you couldn't stand *me*," I blurted out, and then immediately regretted my words. *Smooth move, Barrie,* I told myself. *This is a really clever way to bring up the subject.*

Paul shook his head. I wished I could see his face. "I thought you knew how I felt about you, Barrie," he said. "I thought you were the one who didn't want to be with me."

I couldn't believe what I was hearing. "How could you think that?" I asked in astonishment. "I *loved* being with you, until you started acting like I was polluted or something. It was getting so bad that I was even afraid to say hello to you."

"How about the way *you* acted?" Paul shot back. "That night we went to The Topping, you were embarrassed being with me, weren't you? Because all the girls had dates the size of the Empire State Building, and you were there with somebody you had to look down at!"

I gasped. "Did you think I was ashamed of you?" I asked, dreading the answer. It was true that I *had* been ashamed, for just the briefest of moments. But then I'd remembered what a great guy Paul was, and I hadn't given that stupid girl's comments a second thought. Apparently, though, Paul had—and third and fourth thoughts, too.

"Well, weren't you?" he persisted.

I did my best to explain what had happened that night at The Topping. It was hard to find the words, because I was ashamed of the way I'd reacted. I couldn't believe I'd gotten upset over something so unimportant. It was true that the Barrie who had first come to Rolling Meadows had had all kinds of dumb ideas about what a guy should be. But the Barrie who was here now had learned what was really important. I tried to tell all of this to Paul as we got closer and closer to the farm.

When I finally finished, he peered at me in the mirror. Abruptly he pulled the car to the side of the road and stopped. In one quick motion he got out of the driver's seat and was next to me in the back. Then Paul smiled at me, that same warm smile I'd first seen the day he'd rescued me when Plum Rose ran away. His voice was firm but full of laughter as he said, "Listen, lady. We gave ourselves a lot of misery because we didn't tell each other how we really felt. We're not going to make the same mistake again, got it? We're going to settle all this stuff right now."

I was thrilled. "Oh, yeah?" I teased. "Says who?"

Paul put his arms around me very, very gently. "Says me," he answered. He bent his head, and I felt his lips softly brush mine. He leaned back for a moment and looked at me, and then kissed me again, longer this time and even more sweetly.

I felt dizzy with happiness, but there were still some questions I had to ask. "What about Heather?" I murmured. "I thought you really liked her."

Paul snorted, still holding me close. "You can't be serious. Heather? Come on!"

"Really. We all thought something was going on between the two of you," I argued. "Look at all the time you spent together—"

"—time which we spent talking about nothing but riding," Paul interrupted. "Look, Heather's a licensed exercise rider. She's learned a lot of things I don't know anything about, so I asked her for some tips about the tracks, and she told me. Believe me, Barrie, that is *all* that ever went on between us." He grinned down at me. "Of course, I don't exactly mind that you're a little jealous."

"Who's jealous?" I lied. "I just thought you had better taste than that."

"I do." Paul stroked my hair. "But when you acted like you didn't like me because of my height, it really hurt. I was never attracted to Heather at all, but she acted like I was something special. Whenever you and I were together, it seemed like all we did was fight."

"Not anymore," I promised him, slipping my arms around his neck. "I don't want to fight again for the rest of the summer!" At that moment all I wanted to do was sit in that car forever with Paul's arms wrapped around me.

* * *

It was a terrible shock when my parents called to tell me they'd be taking me home at the end of the week. I almost choked on my dinner when Christy and Harv broke the news. Luckily Dutch had invited Heather to eat with him that night. I didn't want her to hear any of what promised to be a huge family fight.

"Christy, you can't let them do it," I pleaded. "Paul and I just got together. If I leave jockey school now, I'll never see him again."

Harv peered at my leg, which was stretched out in its cast on a spare chair. "And just how are you planning on riding, honey?"

"Don't even ask," Christy advised. "She's so head over heels in love that she'd probably try it with *two* broken legs."

"Now look, guys," I said, "I have a commitment here. Even if I can't exactly ride, I can—"

"What?" Christy asked. "Muck out stalls? Haul bales of hay? You'd probably be a real whiz with a wheelbarrow. Face it, Barrie, until that cast comes off, you are totally unfit for stable work."

"How about if I helped Dutch with his paperwork?" I offered in desperation. "I could do that sitting down in the office."

Christy shook her head. "And if I know you, you'd be trying to convince Dutch to put you back on active duty inside of a week. Forget it, Barrie. I don't want you to be tempted.

Your parents are worried about you, and they want you home. You're out of here as of Friday night."

Boy, that's hospitality for you, I thought bitterly, *kicking me out just because I've had an accident.* But a little voice inside my head whispered that Christy and Harv knew me pretty well. They really were doing this for my own good. It was funny how much louder that little voice had gotten this summer. Maybe that was a good thing, but it didn't help matters at all right now.

The students threw me a farewell party at the stables the day I was scheduled to leave. They'd even gotten me funny little presents. In spite of my glum mood, I loved unwrapping them and finding out what each person thought I really needed. (There was no present from Heather, thank goodness. The only gift I wanted from her was her absence—permanently.)

"A year's supply of emery boards! Thanks, Marla," I said as everyone chuckled.

"Now you won't keep borrowing mine when you break a nail," she laughed.

I held out my hands. Far from being long and polished, as they had been when I'd first arrived, the nails were short and stubby. "Look at this. I don't think I'll ever have a nail to break again!"

Greg and Bobby had chipped in for the

next present. I unwrapped several records of the square-dance music we'd had the night of the barn dance. "You're such a good dancer, I figured you might want to practice with them when you're back on your feet," Greg explained.

"Thanks, guys," I said in delight. "Now all I'll have to do is find partners as good as you to dance with."

Tessa, Jo, and Wendy handed me a smaller box. Inside was a lovely folded piece of silk. "It's for your helmet," Jo explained. "Like the jockeys wear." The silk was emerald green, my favorite color. It was embroidered with the word Champion.

I hugged them all, getting a little misty-eyed as I did. "You guys are just great," I sniffled, but I had another reason for crying. Paul hadn't come to my party. I hoped he wasn't going to let me leave without saying good-bye.

When the party broke up, I slowly made my way on my new crutches to the office, where Dutch was waiting. As I came through the screen door, I saw that he wasn't alone. Paul was with him, and he was grinning from ear to ear, as if he had a wonderful secret he was bursting to share.

"I'm afraid we've got bad news, Barrie," Dutch said, trying to repress a smile.

"What do you mean? What's wrong?" I

demanded, looking from him to Paul. If they had bad news, why were they both so happy?

"Well, it seems your folks won't be able to pick you up today after all," Dutch said, "so Paul has volunteered to give you a lift home."

"Oh, that's terrific!" I cried. It was so thoughtful of Dutch. He knew Paul and I wanted to spend more time together, so he'd given Paul some time off for the drive.

"It'll be nice to have one of your fellow jockeys in the neighborhood, won't it?" Dutch drawled.

I stared at him. "What neighborhood? What are you talking about?"

Grinning even more broadly than before, Paul explained, "Dutch called one of his friends, a trainer who works at Marlborough Raceway. He's agreed to take me on as his assistant. I start the day after tomorrow!"

I couldn't believe it. Instead of saying goodbye to Paul forever, I'd be able to see him almost every day, since Marlborough Raceway was only about ten miles outside of my hometown!

I hobbled over to Dutch and gave him a big kiss. I wanted to kiss Paul, too, but I figured we'd have plenty of time for that later.

Christy and Harv helped Paul pack my gear into the trunk of his car. "Here's all your riding stuff," Christy told me, handing over a nylon duffel bag. "I packed your shoes in there, too."

I peeked inside. Sure enough, the silver dancing shoes lay on top of the pile. "They sure didn't do what I thought they'd do," I said to Christy.

She laughed. "It's funny how things work out sometimes, isn't it? But don't get rid of them. You just might have a chance to wear them again sometime."

I hugged and kissed Christy and Harv. I knew I'd miss them, but I also knew that I'd be coming back often.

Paul looked over at me. "All set?"

"All set," I assured him. He helped me into the car, put my crutches in the backseat, and closed the door. Then he got into the driver's seat. With a last wave at Christy and Harv, we were on our way. My jockey-school summer was over, but my new romance was just beginning.

SWEET DREAMS are fresh, fun and exciting—alive with the flavor of the contemporary teen scene—the joy and doubt of first love. If you've missed any SWEET DREAMS titles, then you're missing out on your kind of stories, written about people like you!

☐	26976	P.S. I LOVE YOU #1 Barbara P. Conklin	$2.75
☐	28348	GOLDEN GIRL #169 Jane Ballard	$2.75
☐	28383	ROCK 'N ROLL SWEETHEART #170 Laurie Lykken	$2.75
☐	28463	ACTING ON IMPULSE #171 Susan Jo Wallach	$2.75
☐	28517	SUNKISSED #172 Stephanie St. Pierre	$2.75
☐	28551	MUSIC FROM THE HEART #173 Pamela L. Laskin	$2.75
☐	28633	LOVE ON STRIKE #174 J. Boies	$2.75
☐	28830	PUPPY LOVE #175 Carla Bracale	$2.75
☐	28840	WRONG-WAY ROMANCE #176 Sherri Cobb	$2.95
☐	28862	THE TRUTH ABOUT LOVE #177 Laurie Lykken	$2.95
☐	28900	PROJECT BOYFRIEND #178 Susan Sloate	$2.95

STARFIRE

Romance Has Never Been So Much Fun!

All-Star Movie and TV Favorites
The Hottest Teen Heartthrobs!

These terrific star bios are packed with the juicy details *you* want to know. Here's the inside scoop on the star's family life, friends, tips on dating, life on the set, future career plans, *plus* fantastic photo inserts.